Praise for *Arch of Bone*

"This is the story Melville should have written."
—Daniel Pinkwater, author of *The Neddiad*

"Yolen's original twist on *Moby-Dick* combines a unique premise with edge-of-your-seat adventure. Fourteen-year-old Josiah is engagingly characterized from the outset as a boy on the edge of manhood, searching for answers about his father's death. Under the arch of bone he has tantalizing dreams of Ahab's hunt for Moby-Dick. A gripping tale by a master storyteller—when I finished it, I started over and read it again."
—Katherine Coville, author of *Briar and Rose and Jack*

"Elemental and timeless. The thrill of Josiah's adventure comes from watching him learn how to survive the wilderness, but it also has much to share about coming to terms with the loss of a parent and humans' complicated relationship to the natural world."
—Eliot Schrefer, National Book Award Finalist

Praise for Jane Yolen

"Jane Yolen facets her glittering stories with the craft of a master jeweller."
—Elizabeth Wein, author of *Code Name Verity*

"There is simply no better storyteller working in the fantasy field today. She's a national treasure."
—Terri Windling, author of *The Wood Wife* and *The Essential Bordertown*

★ "[Yolen] once again delivers the magic, humor, and lovely prose that has attracted readers for years."
—*Library Journal* on *The Emerald Circus*, starred review

★ "These highly entertaining retellings are perfect for teen fans of fairy tales and classic literature.
—*School Library Journal* on *The Emerald Circus*, starred review

"These Tachyon volumes are an invaluable reminder of Yolen's central role in contemporary fantasy, and perhaps an equally invaluable starting point for readers."
—*Locus* on *The Emerald Circus* and *How to Fracture a Fairy Tale*

ARCH OF BONE
JANE YOLEN

Novels
The Wizard of Washington Square (1969)
Hobo Toad and the Motorcycle Gang (1970)
The Bird of Time (1971)
The Magic Three of Solatia (1974)
The Transfigured Hart (1975)
The Mermaid's Three Wisdoms (1978)
The Acorn Quest (1981)
The Stone Silenus (1984)
Cards of Grief (1985)
The Devil's Arithmetic (1988)
The Dragon's Boy (1990)
Wizard's Hall (1991)
Briar Rose (1992)
Good Griselle (1994)
The Wild Hunt (1995)
The Sea Man (1997)
Here There Be Ghosts (1998)
Sword of the Rightful King (2003)
The Young Merlin Trilogy: Passager, Hobby, and Merlin (2004)
Except the Queen (with Midori Snyder, 2010)
Snow in Summer (2011)
Curse of the Thirteenth Fey (2012)
B. U. G. (Big Ugly Guy) (with Adam Stemple, 2013)
Centaur Rising (2014)
A Plague of Unicorns (2014)
Trash Mountain (2015)
The Last Tsar's Dragons (with Adam Stemple, 2019)

Collections
The Girl Who Cried Flowers and Other Tales (1974)
The Moon Ribbon (1976)
The Hundredth Dove and Other Tales (1977)
Dream Weaver (1979)
Neptune Rising: Songs and Tales of the Undersea People (1982)
Tales of Wonder (1983)
The Whitethorn Wood and Other Magicks (1984)
Dragonfield and Other Stories (1985)
Favorite Folktales of the World (1986)
Merlin's Booke (1986)
The Faery Flag (1989)
Storyteller (1992)
Here There Be Dragons (1993)
Here There Be Unicorns (1994)
Here There Be Witches (1995)
Among Angels (with Nancy Willard, 1995)
Here There Be Angels (1996)
Here There Be Ghosts (1998)
Twelve Impossible Things Before Breakfast (1997)
Sister Emily's Lightship and Other Stories (2000)

Not One Damsel in Distress (2000)
Mightier Than the Sword (2003)
Once Upon A Time (She Said) (2005)
The Last Selchie Child (2012)
Grumbles from the Forest: Fairy-Tales Voices with a Twist (with Rebecca Kai Dotlich, 2013)
The Emerald Circus (2017)
How to Fracture a Fairy Tale (2018)
The Midnight Circus (2020)

Graphic Novels
Foiled (2010)
The Last Dragon (2011)
Curses! Foiled Again (2013)

Stone Man Mysteries (with Adam Stemple)
Stone Cold (2016)
Sanctuary (2018)
Breaking Out the Devil (2019)

Young Heroes series (with Robert J. Harris)
Odysseus in the Serpent Maze (2001)
Hippolyta and the Curse of the Amazons (2002)
Atalanta and the Arcadian Beast (2003)
Jason and the Gorgon's Blood (2004)

Pit Dragon Chronicles Series
Dragon's Blood (1982)
Heart's Blood (1984)
A Sending of Dragons (1988)
Dragon's Heart (2009)

Tartan Magic
The Wizard's Map (1999)
The Pictish Child (1999)
The Bagpiper's Ghost (2002)

Books of the Great Alta
Sister Light, Sister Dark (1988)
White Jenna (1989)
The One-Armed Queen (1998)

A Rock 'n' Roll Fairy Tale Series
Pay the Piper (With Adam Stemple, 2005)
The Troll Bridge (With Adam Stemple, 2006)
Boots and the Seven Leaguers (2000)

The Seelie Wars Series (with Adam Stemple)
The Hostage Prince (2013)
The Last Changeling (2014)
The Seelie King's War (2016)

Arch *of Bone*

Jane Yolen

Illustrated by Ruth Sanderson

TACHYON

SAN FRANCISCO

Interior and cover design by Elizabeth Story
Illustrations and cover art by Ruth Sanderson
Author photo © 2015 by Jason Stemple

Tachyon Publications LLC
1459 18th Street #139
San Francisco, CA 94107
415.285.5615
www.tachyonpublications.com
tachyon@tachyonpublications.com

Series editor: Jacob Weisman
Project editor: Jaymee Goh

Print ISBN: 978-1-61696-350-7
Digital ISBN: 978-1-61696-351-4

Printed in the United States by Versa Press, Inc.

First Edition: 2021
9 8 7 6 5 4 3 2 1

For Peter B. Tacy:

Steadfast sailor, one-time Commodore of the Stonington Harbor Yacht Club, teacher and poet who has sailed these channels and moored himself in me. He has brought sea and islands into my life, and given me much valuable sailing/wind/charts/recovery advice. I have named Josiah's boat after one of PBT's own. Any mistakes in seamanship in this book are my own.—JY

Foreword

More than twenty-five miles off the coast of Massachusetts, Nantucket is a smallish island, only fourteen miles long. Today Nantucket is a summer tourist island. I have visited it several times. But during a brief period in the late eighteenth and early nineteenth centuries, it was the whaling capital of the world and, as such, one of the wealthiest places in America. And then petroleum was found as a much better and easier power source. Whaling ceased to be the wealth-maker and, for the most part, was abandoned.

This book is set in that place and that time, and its major motivator was the novel *Moby-Dick*. Written by Herman Melville, *Moby-Dick* has been a favorite of mine since I first read it in high school. It is a highly romanticized novel of the brutal life of whalers on the sea that was loosely based on an actual event in

1819—when the whaleship *Essex* was destroyed by a tremendous spermaceti whale who was—in the newspaper accounts of the day, a pure white.

Possibly the whale was a female. Like elephants, spermaceti whales—better known as sperm whales— are matriarchal. The females raise the young whales in large groups, or pods, babysitting and even suckling one another's calves. It is well known that they will act—singly or collectively—to protect all of the young whales. So, it's quite possible that the spermaceti whale that twice rammed the *Essex* and sent it to the bottom of the ocean was a female, intent only on keeping the pod and the babies safe. Not—as Moby-Dick is in the book—a vengeful male out to kill the intemperate Captain Ahab who had left a harpoon in his back, and at the same time kill Ahab's crew as well.

In the book even the good man, First Mate Starbuck, is not spared. Only one, a simple sailor who clings to a floating wooden coffin, is saved. In fact, the novel *Moby-Dick* begins with the sentence "Call me Ishmael," as the surviving sailor addresses the reader of the book.

Melville's novel *Moby-Dick* was based on a real event. However, my book follows those left behind in Melville's telling—the widow Starbuck and her son Josiah. It is their story, or rather Josiah's story, because that has not been told up to this time. My book borrows characters and setting from Melville's book, but looks at them from a different perspective. Some characters are the same, some of the settings are different. Occasionally I borrowed scenes or reset scenes elsewhere, and these appear in the dream sequences. But you will find a lot of literary hand-shaking going on here.

I hope you have a splendid and safe Nantucket sleigh ride reading this book.

Jane Yolen
October 2020

Leviathan . . . maketh a path
to shine after him
—Job 41:32

CHAPTER ONE:
Knock on the Door

Josiah heard the knock on the front door and shuddered. It was early morning and he had been up well before dawn, bringing in the firewood. Such a knock, so early in the morning, could only mean bad news, awful news, the worst. A whaler's family was always braced for such news, but never really ready for it.

He wondered if he should awaken his mother, then decided against it. She had been sick for several weeks and needed the rest. A winter catarrh still plagued her. She spent the long nights coughing and sometimes spiking a fever, and he was loath to disturb her now.

Rising from the hearth where he'd been stacking the wood, he hurried to the door with a reluctant heart, as if by getting there before his mother, he could take whatever blow was meant for her.

He flung open the door.

Standing on the stone stoop, the late spring sun behind him, was a wild-looking man, his face almost as copper-colored as an old rubbed coin. Clearly a man who had spent days at sea. His hair stood out in startled, curled yellow wisps.

The man's eyes were narrowed as if from too many days staring out across the horizon line of a merciless sea. Those eyes were red-rimmed, haunted. He did not look like a man who often laughed. What he did look like was the sailors who served on whaling vessels, only somewhat better dressed. Indeed, he dressed as if he might have been at sea at one time but now worked in the town.

But which island? Surely not Nantucket, or Josiah would have known him. Nantucket was *that* small.

And what job had he held? That, too, was difficult to tell.

Without his willing it, Josiah's right hand strayed to his belt, where the fishing knife and marlinspike sat snugly tucked away in their leather sheath. His father had given it to him on his tenth birthday, saying, "Thee is old enough, Josiah, to have thine own knife and marlinspike for fishing, but not for any other purpose."

Being a good Quaker boy, Josiah certainly understood. They were never to be used as weapons. But it was still such an important gift, he never felt dressed without it.

"Yes?" Josiah said, forgetting his manners—in the moment before his life would change forever. "Who is calling at such an hour? And have you a name?"

The man held his cap in his right hand. It trembled slightly. His other hand grasped the handles of a cheap but new carpetbag. He said, as if unsure of it, "Call me Ishmael." Then he added, "Ishmael Black. Is this the Starbuck home? I was told in the village that it was."

Josiah nodded, all the while thinking that this Ishmael's voice was like the tolling of a bell. Deep. Resonant. Dangerous.

And, as it turned out, it was.

"Only survivor of a whaling ship," Ishmael continued, putting his hand out to be shaken, but Josiah did not offer him the same greeting in return, for his right hand—along with all his other extremities—had suddenly turned cold.

"Her name," the man continued, "was *Pequod*. I called her my Yale and my Harvard, for I learned all of life and death on her deck, before she was broken apart by that devilfish, that white leviathan, that whale known as Moby-Dick." The man spoke quickly, as if he'd rehearsed what he was going to say for long hours till he had the words right, though not the proper sentiment or voice, for his voice was icy, stark.

The Pequod!

That was when Josiah knew—knew for certain—that his father was dead. Though he and his mother had guessed such might be true, they'd not spoken of it.

"To speak of disaster," his mother often said, "invites it." That was something often quoted in Nantucket and other whaling towns.

There had been no news for so long. Just that the ship was missing.

And they were given many reasons why a ship might not return to port on time. Especially a whaler. For if a whaler had been having a good season, or having a bad time around the Horn on its way home—where the weather was always unpredictable at best—the *Pequod* might have stayed longer at sea, even without a disaster.

This was something his mother had emphasized all winter. So, they had waited. As they waited still. Until this moment.

Josiah didn't move, didn't gesture the man inside, didn't even acknowledge what had just been said. *How do I know I can trust this haunted-eyed stranger?* he thought. *Is he who he claims to be? If he is not Ishmael Black, sole survivor of the* Pequod, *why else might he be here?*

Josiah bit his lower lip. Then, as if inviting a dreadful ghost into the house, he stood aside without a word. It was a poor invitation. Not friendly at all. And for a Friend, a birthright Quaker, that was all but a sin.

Even worse, without meaning to, he curled his right hand over the sheathed knife and marlinspike.

Just then he heard his mother's voice behind him, thin but honest. It did not even tremble, though surely she had heard what Ishmael Black had said:

Sole survivor of the Pequod. The house was too small to disguise such news.

"Come in, then. Thee must have been a long while traveling."

Traveling from Hell, Josiah thought, and wondered why he'd thought that.

Nodding, the man took a step forward. Josiah had to turn entirely sideways to get out of his way.

From the hearth, nearly in the ashes, their dog Ezekiel made a long, low growl at the man but did not otherwise move. Zeke was a good reader of intent, or so Josiah's father often said.

"Is thee staying somewhere nearby?" his mother asked.

Josiah wondered that she was so calm, as if she had already buried her husband and left off mourning. She was not even still coughing. Had the bald announcement of his father's death proved a miracle cure?

"Just come from New Bedford, ma'am, where I once had to share a bed with a cannibal. I thought I'd find a better bed here at the Tucket Inn," the man replied. "Besides, I knew it would be closer to First Mate Starbuck's house."

The Tucket was a small waterfront inn, a humble, besmoked place. Josiah had gone once as a child with his father when, as first mate of a different whaler, his father had to roust out some of the tars for his ship. Once only.

Josiah had been just five and a half at the time, and frantic to be with his father before the first mate shipped off again. But at such a young age, and prone to vivid dreams anyway, Josiah had screamed with a nightmare that night, for some of the men had been covered with scary tattoos, though at the time he had no name for such things.

One of the men leaped out of bed naked, holding a harpoon the size of a giant's spear, and another— equally undressed—wore a necklace made of shrunken human heads. Josiah and his mother and father all slept in bedclothes. He could make no sense of the naked men. In fact, he got it in his head that they meant to eat him.

But once the men were made to understand that the man in Quaker gray was only looking for sailors, everything was fine. Father had seemed unperturbed by them. This was simply part of his job, as he carefully explained to Josiah on their way home. The scary men weren't scary at all but good sailors and fantastic harpooners, the best. And they lived in warm climates where they needed no bedclothes.

But that explanation had not stopped the nightmare that night until Mother had explained the tattoos to him, and reminded him that all people were made in

God's image. And then he had wanted a tattoo himself, but she said he was way too young.

His mother had scarcely forgiven his father for taking him there, though forgiveness was a chief Quaker virtue. And his mother, as clerk of the Nantucket Friends Meeting, should have had "forgiveness" at the top of her daily list.

In fact, as Josiah's nightmares continued, she ragged on his father for months. "Thee should have prepared thy son for such a surprise," she said. "He has been long cossetted, and needed information before going to a sailor's tavern rooming house."

Perhaps, Josiah thought, his distrust of Ishmael Black harkened back to those miserable nights. He would search his heart. Give the man more time.

"That miserly house?" his mother said to the visitor. "'Tis no place for one of thy breeding. I know an educated voice when I hear it, Ishmael Black. A teacher, are ye?"

"Librarian, ma'am," he answered quickly.

Rather too quickly, Josiah thought. He was determined not to like the man and to find fault even if there was none. Almost immediately he thought: *So much for giving Ishmael Black more time.*

"Or rather," Ishmael added, as if it made no difference, "I have worked in a rich patron's library, shelving his books. And sometimes I read deep in them when he would let me. Other times I read *to* him, both works of fiction and law treatises, for his eyes were of little use to him in his old age, no matter how rich he was. I had learned my letters as a young child from my own father, who worked evenings cleaning the church, after the chores on his own farm were done."

"I rather thought so," Josiah's mother said. "Then thee shall stay with us. We Quakers encourage men to better themselves. We should all become our better angels." She glanced over at Josiah when she said that.

But knowing his mother well, Josiah expected she would also think long on it herself and speak of it next First Day at Meeting.

She drew a careful breath, being sure to control any lingering coughs from the catarrh. "We have an extra bed in the loft. We shall be glad of thy company, and that way thee can tell us thy tale, awful as I am sure it is. Librarians have a way with stories. And we would be grateful for the details, as they are certain to be the last we shall know."

At first Josiah thought there was a twinkle in her eye as she spoke, as if the tale she was demanding were a fancy, with talking fishes and three wishes, the kind she used to tell him at bedtime when he was a boy.

But in fact, looking closer, he could see the twinkle was really unshed tears. For the first time, he realized that his mother was weeping, but inwardly. She was Nantucket-bred, a goodly Quaker, steadfast and strong. She settled the accounts and ran the household during all her husband's long trips away at sea. She would not shame his death now with tears shed in front of a stranger.

Nor in front of me. But damn the man who has brought her to such a pass, Josiah thought, suddenly realizing he wasn't certain if he meant damn this Ishmael, or the ship's captain, or—in fact—his own father.

Then he immediately swallowed the curse, his cheeks blushing hot at the thought, and also at the un-Quakerly use of the Biblical word *damn*.

"The boy looks like Starbuck," Ishmael said abruptly, meaning it a compliment, or so Josiah begrudgingly supposed.

Actually, most people said he looked like his mother. He had her slim build, combined with his father's pure, tight skin. Also, he had his mother's rosy cheeks and blushed far too often for a boy. *More like a schoolgirl*, Josiah thought, especially under the librarian/sailor's scrutiny. At fourteen, such a blush was a liability. His friends already teased him unmercifully about it.

"Thee comes with news of my father's death and talks of my looks?" Josiah knew his sudden fury was evident, feeling the blush on his cheeks and trembling of his hands.

"Josiah, mind thy manners," his mother warned.

"Anger is a sin against thyself. Thee knows that Ish- mael Black is a stranger here in a strange land, and we must . . ."

Josiah did not stay to hear more, for suddenly the house seemed much too small for him and filled with a strange black mist that confused his eyes. He felt he might choke on it. So, turning, he ran out the open door and into the brisk Nantucket air, with loyal Zeke bounding after him.

CHAPTER TWO:
The Walk into Town

Heading past the closely clustered wooden houses, as stern and unadorned as their Quaker masters, Josiah raced down the cobblestoned street.

He passed by the three brick houses built by his great-great-uncle Joseph Starbuck, a man rich from whale oil, rich enough to build those houses for his three sons. But none for the other Starbucks, like Josiah's grandfather, who had to climb the shipboard ranks and live on the flanks of the town, not in it.

Not that either his grandfather or father complained. Though his grandmother always had plenty to say about it.

He raced to the harbor, which was flanked by low rope banisters on either side. From the corner of his eye, he could see the row of windmills on the rise above the town, catching the sea breezes in their long arms.

The place was so familiar that he hardly had to blink to take it all in. He had known this spit of land from the time he had been born, had taken his first steps out on the Nantucket pier.

Familiar, and suddenly too close, the town and its island were like twin beasts clawing at his throat, even out here in the tangy air, heavy with the stench of whale oil. If he had to, he could have walked these paths at night without a lamp, or even in the deepest fog, and never lose his way. But somehow it was not where he wanted to be.

Setting the town to his back, Josiah went quickly to the point opposite, where sheep ranged freely on common land. He kept Zeke at his heel with a command. The last thing he needed was for the dog to run off someone's sheep.

When he was far enough away from where anyone might see him, he flung himself onto the wet salt grass and began to sob, never minding that his shirt and trousers would be stained and drenched, and that he was shivering with the cold of the early spring winds.

Cries retched out of him as if they had traveled a long way, almost as far as had Ishmael Black on his way back to Nantucket with his dreaded news.

Zeke was clearly upset by the unusual sound. Josiah had not wept since he was a very small child, and then only in those dreams. Having no other notion of what to do, Zeke kept licking Josiah's neck, pawing at his arms, till Josiah had to turn and bury his face in the dog's rough coat, which made Zeke tremble even more with the unfamiliar emotion and sound.

There they lay for a while, neither one comforted by the baaing of the sheep, or the rustle of lambs gamboling in the new grass. The two of them, dog and boy, barely even heard the crass cries of gulls above.

Josiah tried not to think about his father, but the pictures came fast into his mind: Father laughing as he told a story; Father in Meeting, standing up and trembling while speaking the Lord's message; Father hunched over a piece of whalebone scrimshaw, picking away at it with his knife, creating a picture of three men and a cabin boy on a Nantucket sleigh ride, their small boat being towed by the whale many times larger than a team of oxen.

That scrimshaw sat on their mantelpiece. Josiah's mother always showed it off to visitors. *She is probably handing it to Ishmael Black right now,* he thought, though finding little comfort in that.

Suddenly, all the mental pictures of his father were washed away with the imagined slapping sound of a great white whale's flukes upon the water, which summoned up a whole new round of sobs, another flood of tears, another fierce face-washing by Zeke's rough tongue.

And until this day, I had not even known there was such a thing as a white leviathan, a white whale.

It took some while before he was done with his sobbing, and Zeke kept by his side the entire time. The dog's dark eyes were limpid, wet, as if he, too, had been crying.

At last Josiah sat up. "Enough, Zeke!" he said, then scrubbed his shirtsleeve over his eyes to wipe away the tears. His stomach ached with sorrow, his throat raw with it, as if he had caught his mother's catarrh.

And now his nose was running like a spring flood. The linen sleeve did for that as well.

He guessed his cheeks were patchy and red with crying. *Like a girl's,* he thought, and shuddered. *Like a little girl's!* Though most of the girls he knew from town and from Meeting would have rather died before weeping in company. Hardy they were. Like his mother. Like their mothers. Like any girl in a sailor's family who had a father or brother out somewhere on the sea.

Suddenly Josiah felt the cold. Surely he should go home. Stacking the firewood was not yet done. The cow would need milking. The chickens had not been fed nor their eggs gathered. His father had counted on him, called him "the house's man whilst I am away."

Yet how could he go back now, with his cheeks runneled with tears, and his eyes as bloated as a drowned sailor's?

That unfortunate image made him cry all over again, snuffling and drizzling like a sick child.

Zeke danced about Josiah's feet in an agony of indecision before a single ram ran in front of them, and he took off after it.

"Zeke, to me," Josiah cried out, and the dog stopped in his tracks, reluctantly turning about. Then, shamefaced, he made his way back to his young master. They both turned and walked down to the sea, leaving the confused ram to find its own way back to the flock.

A wandering ewe came close to them on the path, her dark face innocent of all knowledge, but she skittered away when they got near.

Zeke trembled this time and did not follow her. Instead he stuck close to Josiah until they got to the water.

Josiah made an inarticulate sound, somewhere between a cry and a moan, then waded into the ocean till his boots were half covered. All the while, Zeke stayed on shore, preferring solid land to the movement of water.

Poor dog, Josiah thought, *he'd almost drowned as a pup*

and had never been happy in a boat since. He plunged his hands into the water, splashing it on his face. The salt stung his eyes, got up his nose.

He made another sound, this time like a horse. But the water had done its cold work, shocking him back into himself.

Slowly he waded back to shore, then walked into town, keeping his mind a careful blank, like a child's first school slate. He almost did not hear his name called out by several of the boys down on the pier who'd been watching for the whalers to come in. Nor did he notice old Abram Quary walk by, the last man on Nantucket with Indian blood, who usually spoke to the Nantucket boys but never to the women or girls.

Josiah did not even count the whaling ships as was his wont, rolling their names on his tongue like a great epic poem, bound as they were for the Pacific waters: ships like the *Martha*, the *Baltic*, the *Equator*. Nor did he bob his head to the gray-skirted women from Meeting, who greeted him familiarly along the narrow crooked main street.

Instead he looked out at the great dark Atlantic, rolling its waves towards the shore, as if herding them, their caps white with foam.

As he stared off to the horizon, where the sun struggled to win release from its prison of clouds,

Josiah wondered where in the cold, dark grave of the other ocean his father's body rolled.

My father's body, he thought, and shuddered. Probably still dressed in the greatcoat that he'd bought after his first sailing, many years earlier, and the boots Grandfather Starbuck—a ship's captain himself—had given his son when he'd first declared for the sea.

At this moment, there was only one thing Josiah was sure of: If his father's body was truly out there, anchored in its death by the heavy water, his soul had been set free and was even now in the mariner's heaven where he still sought the great whales and sang out about the beauty and bounty of God's enduring gifts.

Because that is what Father is like, Josiah thought, then amended the thought quickly. *What he was like.*

He said a short prayer, but not out loud.

Suddenly, he had another, more pressing worry: *Mother needs me at home.* He thought of her there at the house: her decency and commitment to the Quaker way leading her to reach out to this Ishmael Black, to treat him as a friend.

Even in her despair at his message, she still felt the need to keep Ishmael Black close, to offer him sustenance and a place to sleep while he spun out all the details of her beloved husband's death. And the death of all his friends. Harrowing, horrible details.

Yes! Josiah thought, *that is it. Not something else. She is bringing him comfort, which it tells us to do in God's Bible. Comfort the afflicted.*

And then he thought: *I have no such need. Dead is dead. Whether Father died by a whale or by falling from the mast or by the hands of a treacherous captain matters little. He is still dead. Before his time. Before he made captain.* Josiah's grandfather and all those Starbuck grandfathers before them had been captains. And all of them comfortably dead in their beds at great ages, with their children and grandchildren around them to say their farewells.

And then he thought, miserably, *Father died before he had his own ship. Before I had a final moment to tell him how much I loved him.*

And with that furious moment of self-recognition, Josiah turned his back to the harbor, set his face to the house, and began to make his quick way up the walk to home.

He hoped to God that Ishmael Black was long gone, to the Tucket Inn, or, preferably, farther. Maybe back to New Bedford, on the mainland. *Anywhere,* Josiah thought, *but having tea and biscuits with Mother at the Starbuck house.*

But that wish, like many others to come, was not to be granted.

CHAPTER THREE:
The Long Visit

Josiah returned to the house when it was past luncheon and heading towards evening—both he and the dog huffing from the walk. When he opened the door, Josiah was not pleased. Nor was he particularly surprised to see that the seaman was still sitting rather too familiarly at the table, as if neither Ishmael Black nor his mother had moved since Josiah had left hours before, though he could see the remains of one or maybe two meals on the table.

There was a platter with crumbs and a single slice of his mother's butter bread on it, plus half a jar of her blueberry jam. This was odd, for his mother—as often described by his father—was house proud. "Sometimes," his father had teased, "she clears the dishes before we are done eating!"

Furthermore, Josiah's mother was about to pour

what was surely a fifth or sixth new cup of tea for Ishmael Black. She had poised the teapot at its apogee and was staring right at Josiah.

"Josiah?" she said, as if anyone else would have entered the house without knocking. "I was beginning to wonder where thee had gotten to," she finished, as the tea began to waterfall into Ishmael Black's cup, and after that, into her own.

"Clearing my head," Josiah told her curtly. "The dog's, too." He was glad his shirt and trousers had dried even before the walk home and he hadn't been tasked about it, which would have been an embarrassment to all.

"Lads' heads often need clearing," Ishmael remarked. "As surely did mine at such an age. But shipping off to sea for me was one way of dealing with such head-clearings. Nothing like a good easterly to . . ."

"Thee were hardly a lad then," Josiah said, mostly under his breath.

Only his mother seemed to notice Josiah's biting rejoinder, for the seaman was following up his own remark by saying, "I was just about to tell your mother what truly happened on the day we spotted the white whale." He seemed to have little appreciation for anyone else's voice.

Josiah refrained from pointing out that Ishmael had already been several hours closeted with the widow

Starbuck. He could have told her an entire whaling saga in leisurely fashion in that time. But one part of Josiah was glad that his mother would not have to hear the story of her husband's death for a second time in its fullest version without him there for comfort.

But instead of saying so, he just went to the cupboard for a bowl in which to put water for Zeke and a teacup and plate for himself. He felt famished. Going hungry rarely happened in his house, for his mother liked to cook.

Reaching across the table, he grabbed up a knife and the slice of bread and quickly slathered it with the jam. Then he took a huge bite, swallowing it almost whole. Sitting, he turned to his mother and said, "I am ready if Mother can bear to hear it all. But I can tell thee, Ishmael Black, without fear of contradiction, that thee will get little thanks for thy recitation after."

His mother did not interrupt this exchange, for as clerk of the local Meeting, she'd had much practice in when to contradict and when to let silence guide her tongue. But she poured yet another cup of tea, this one for Josiah, as if it were a warning, before saying, "We will have a prayer and then we will eat." Then she added, "Where was thy prayer before eating, Josiah?"

It was not the question he was expecting. He looked down at the crumbs on the table, at the half-eaten slice of jammy bread. Then, stretching out his hand over them, he muttered, "For what we are about to receive, thank thee, Lord."

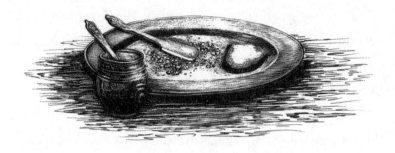

"Tardy but still meaningful," she said, touching his head lightly. It was meant as a scold, but they had both needed that touch. He looked up into her eyes and saw forgiveness and love.

She spoke to them both, saying, "An early dinner, for I dare guess, Josiah, that thee has had no midday meal. And no breakfast, as I recall. But as I work on the preparation, good Ishmael Black, please get on with the tale. Not the whole of it. I will not want to sleep upon the ending. But at least the beginning, so that we can all rest without nightmares this night."

Josiah nodded but said nothing more, thankful for his mother's keen senses and keener close confidences. But he did wonder what she and Ishmael Black had to say to one another if he had not told her the tale without her son there. Perhaps they had been discussing the rich man's library or books they had both read. Or perhaps she had told him about Nantucket and its citizens, or schooled him on its history. Or . . . It all made his head spin.

"I do not need thanks," Ishmael Black said politely, setting his cup down before him. Then he folded his hands together, lacing his long fingers as if in prayer, before beginning to tell the tale.

"I shall not start from the earliest arrivals," he said, "for it began—so I was assured by my new compatriots—the way all whaling voyages did, with men from many lands coming together. Though I must especially mention my cannibal friend, a man of many tattoos and much heart, named Queequeg. He hailed from an island far away called Rokokovo, if I have that right, for he was always correcting my accent. There he was a prince, though not at all like any princes you might have met in a fairy tale set in England or France. Or not even like the princes in the Bible. I read many of those stories to the old man whose library I tended, especially at night, before he could finally go to sleep. He called me his Shakespeare, though I had written not a word of any of them."

He took a quick breath, too quick for either Josiah or his mother to get a word in, finishing with, "It was Queequeg who, all unintentioned, saved my life.

Though he lost his own in the process."

He's making it up, Josiah thought. *A cannibal* friend? *I wish he'd eaten this Ishmael Black up before they ever got on board the* Pequod.

But a part of him believed every word. He'd seen what kinds of crews the whaling ships carried. And men from the cannibal isles were reputed to be great harpooners used to sailing from isle to isle for their food. He recalled the scary men at the inn, who had given him nightmares when he was a child.

"Queequeg and I . . ." Ishmael Black continued, ". . . met in New Bedford, and in the morning sailed aboard a small packet to your lovely island, and it so neat and tight and tidy, and smelling of sea and blubber and oil." He smiled. His teeth were very white against his sun-scorched skin, and his eyes were dark as storm clouds. "I especially appreciated the Quaker ladies like small gray doves walking in quick pairs and threes along the quayside. Why, Mrs. Starbuck . . ." Ishmael said, cocking his head to one side.

Like a courting bird, Josiah thought, and shivered.

"Perhaps," Ishmael Black said to Josiah's mother, "one of them was you." He giggled like a schoolboy, which made Josiah shudder. But not noticing the distance on Josiah's face or the shudder, Ishmael went on. "And the boys still too young to ship out on their own, like Josiah here, but not uninterested in watching real sailors at work, were a fine sight, too." Now he nodded at Josiah, who shrugged at Ishmael's awkward attempt at including him.

If Ishmael was dismayed at the shrug or even saw it, he gave no sign but continued his slow way towards the meat of the story.

And all the while Josiah's left leg, well hidden beneath the table, was trembling, as if little fish swam inside his trousers. Josiah wanted desperately for Ishmael Black to get on with the story and at the same time did not want to hear what he had to say. Did not—as his mother did not—want to sleep soon after the story ended.

"And thence Queequeg the cannibal and I walked farther to find our ship," Ishmael Black said, showing no sign that he had spotted Josiah's impatience at all. "We passed by two others bound for three-year voyages—the *Tit-Bit*, and the *Devil-Dam*. Both burdened with unfortunate names, I thought, and Queequeg thought the same. 'Do not name your ship death names,'" he said in an odd, strangely accented, guttural voice, which Josiah suddenly realized was an attempt to sound like the cannibal. "Do not suggest it is too small to make the voyage," Ishmael finished, with a flourish of his right hand.

"Ah," Josiah's mother replied, half a sigh, half permission to continue.

"We settled on the third, the whaler called *Pequod*. It was a rare old ship of the old school, both quaint and grotesque at the same time. It put me in mind of some of the odd castles I had seen in my travels, before I became the librarian . . ."

"Old Peleg's ship!" Josiah cried, unable to stop himself. "It *is* a rarity. And yes, my father set sail on that one." Then he remembered that Ishmael Black had already mentioned the *Pequod* when the door had first opened to him. It made Josiah feel like a simpleton, too stupid to hold more than one thought in his head at a time. He shut his mouth as if it were a rat trap.

His mother put a hand on his arm, a caution to his enthusiasm, as if to remind him why they were there, what they were to listen for.

Encouraged by both responses, Ishmael Black opened up further, like a ship raising sail. "And my! There is a lot of work in preparing to go out to sea, as I am certain you know. Lifting and loading, a great deal of scrubbing of decks, and learning to attend to the various moods of the captain and first mate. The one being a grandiose old dog of the sea called Ahab, a name as Biblical, Josiah, as yours or mine. You may not know it, but Ahab was the seventh king of Israel, a wicked, weak man who worshipped Baal, and lived under the thumb of his harridan wife called Jezebel, according to Hebrew scriptures. She was thrown from a window by men pledged to Jehovah and—"

"And eaten by dogs," Josiah put in, interrupting the man's long narrative diversion, all the while thinking: *If this seaman-librarian believes Quaker boys do not know their Bible, both parts,* that *should disabuse him of the notion.*

But it turned out nothing could deter Ishmael Black from embroidering his tale, or from filling it with asides, and asides on those asides, along the way.

"One has to wonder what the captain's parents were thinking, to name a child so," he added smoothly. "Now, Josiah, your namesake was a different sort of Hebrew king, and—"

"Josiah is named for his grandfather," his mother said with that firm edge she had occasionally used with his father; he'd sometimes paid little heed to his listeners. And sometimes she used that tone as clerk of Meeting for the same reasons. Ishmael Black heard the caution and was, for a moment, silent.

Josiah rushed into the empty space, saying: "Father would sometimes go on too long, too," which suddenly cut like a knife, for he would never hear his father tell tales, short or long, again. That reminder lay heavy as an anvil on his shoulders.

His mother got up without speaking, boiled more water, refreshened the teapot, and filled the cups again. Then she got out another loaf of brown bread from the pantry, and a second pot of jam, made from last year's blueberries, which had been a bumper crop all across the island. All this in order to give their visitor time to resettle into his tale.

The ice in the room was felt by all three of them, but none spoke of it. Instead the seaman threw himself back into the story, as if hoping it would clear the room of one kind of tension with the introduction of another.

"This Captain Ahab was a hard man, made harder by the fact that he bore a deep wound. His right leg was fashioned out of ivory for—it was said by the captain himself—a great white whale had bitten it off, nearly killing him. And he had sworn a great oath on the Bible itself that he would make that leviathan pay for what it had done."

Josiah thought such an oath wrong and did not have to wait long for his mother's response. He had heard it often enough when she counseled at Meeting.

"'Vengeance,'" she said right on cue, "'is mine, saith the Lord.'"

"Well," Ishmael Black answered with what he surely thought was a winning smile, "on a ship the captain *is* lord of all things. So, it cannot be counted as ordinary vengeance."

That shocked the room into a brutal silence, but Josiah was pleased, thinking: *Now she knows who and what this man is.* He expected her to respond with something like *"Even kings are laid low in the Testaments . . ."* But instead she said, "Friend Ishmael, often I have heard my husband say such a thing. And often have I admonished him for it. There is only the one God and we are poor imitations. But still we must try. I urge *thee* to try harder as well. Listen to that small, still voice inside thee, which some call conscience and some call God. *Thee* may not be a Quaker, but in this house, thee shall act like one."

She stood abruptly. "Tomorrow we shall hear more of thy story. I am not yet ready in my soul to receive this information. I will begin the supper preparations now. Josiah, I will need three eggs from the hens. It will be a small repast. See what vegetables be out in the garden. Check the cellar for potatoes and apples."

Josiah was glad that she had not sent Ishmael off to do his chores. He took it as a sign that he was still the man of the house and got up at once without a single protest.

Before he could get through the door, he heard his mother say to Ishmael Black, "Meanwhile, there is a bed through that door and up the stairs, to the left of the pantry, ready-made for any visitor who should need it. I urge thee to thine own prayers, whatever they may be. Thee might wish to say a prayer and nap till suppertime. Or take a walk down to the shore and back, whichever is thy wont. I will pray that thy dreams are softer than the ones thee may have had on the sea."

With that, she cleared the table and set to washing the dishes in the sink, her back turned sturdily to the two of them.

Josiah knew *that* back well enough. Ishmael would have to learn it if he wanted to stay much longer. But Josiah did not need to remark upon it. His mother's stiffened back said it all.

Clearly, Ishmael understood, and silently left to go to his room. Josiah stopped to give his mother a small hug before heading out. She shooed him away with her hand, as she often did, and he was not surprised.

The chickens had been reluctant to give up their eggs at such a late hour, but Josiah persevered. The garden still had a few old peas. He found two leftover potatoes and three leftover apples in the cellar. He brought them in to his mother, who was delighted with everything.

When the three returned for supper, they ate in what might have been a companionable silence if it hadn't carried so much weight. Josiah felt it in his breastbone, an ache that would not go away.

Soon after finishing his meal, which Ishmael Black

ate like a librarian and not a famished seaman, he thanked them both profusely. Then pleading weariness, he returned to his room.

But Josiah, as part of the work that his father had left to him, helped with the dishes, fed the dog, put the chickens in their runs, and stoked the fire in the hearth to keep the house warm for the first part of the night. April nights in Nantucket could still be quite cold. Then he went to his room and lay down.

Josiah had no idea what the seaman would dream about that night. But when he said his own prayers, Josiah was not surprised to find they were messages to his dead father: mostly promises to take better care of his mother, now that he knew he was *truly* the man of the house. At least he hoped that would prove true for quite some time.

CHAPTER FOUR:

A Day Longer Than the Day Before

Josiah woke to a brilliant morning, the dawn chorus of birds like a choir, and his mother singing in the kitchen, which he had not heard for the last six months, when they'd been told by Captain Peleg, owner of the *Pequod,* that the boat was missing and that he knew no more facts than that.

That she could sing this morning, knowing Father was dead, truly astonished Josiah. She should have been weeping. Or at least sighing.

Josiah got dressed and put on his First Day shoes even though it wasn't First Day, and there was no Quaker meeting. Then he put the sheathed knife and marlinspike on his belt. He wanted to honor his father and knew no other way to do it, even though the sheath fit poorly on the wider belt.

As he left his room, he heard another voice join his

mother's in the song. A voice he didn't immediately recognize. Higher than his father's booming baritone, lighter, less substantial, but certainly more in key.

It took him a moment before he realized it was that seaman, that interloper, that teller of tales who seemed to know the song well enough to even provide harmony.

Harmony! Josiah gagged at the thought, when what Ishmael had brought into the house was disharmony, sadness, and fear.

He went back into his bedroom, sat down angrily on the bed, tore off the First Day Shoes, and pulled on his worn everyday pair. He put the old knife and marlinspike, still in their worn sheath, on the old belt, where they sat more comfortably than in his Meeting clothes.

When he came into the kitchen, both singers turned as one, but only his mother stopped singing.

She smiled at Josiah, nodded, then turned back to setting the table. For three.

Meanwhile, Ishmael leaned back against the wall and kept the song going. It was a light country air that Josiah did not know.

"Waley, waley," the seaman-librarian sang, and then finished the verse before sitting down at the table.

Josiah knew from the lyrics that the song was not about whales at all, but about lost love. Not love lost to death, but to abandonment. Why his mother had been singing that was not a surprise. She often sang when disturbed. But that Ishmael Black should have joined her in the singing was, at the very least, inappropriate.

Breakfast was an uncomfortable and silent affair, though the seaman tried several times to start a conversation. But Josiah and his mother, both practiced in Quaker silence, were not to be drawn out.

"If thee has nothing good to say," his mother often cautioned, "best not say anything at all."

But once the simple meal of porridge was done with, and the seaman's praise of it—"Much better than sailor's tack!"—had settled like fog in the air, they cleared the table and washed the dishes and cutlery, all in a kind of agreed-upon silence. When that was done, Josiah's mother turned to the seaman.

"Shall we hear the rest of thy tale in daylight?" she asked, her voice soft but calm. "And no need to tell us all, just the whale part. I am a first mate's wife." There was a soft catch in her breath. "Well, widow, as it seems. In my long years, I have heard many stories about the preparations for whaling journeys. They vary little in substance, though oft in their particulars.

And to be ever truthful, my dear new friend in God, I am not certain I could sit through it knowing how the story must end."

Ishmael Black had the grace to nod in understanding. "I will get to the story's point, then, Mrs. Starbuck. But remember, this captain was not out for just *any* whale. He was specifically out for the great white leviathan, the one he called 'Moby-Dick.' If you forget this one thing, the tale would only be 'full of sound and fury and signifying nothing,' as the great poet says."

"'Tis not in the Bible," she remarked.

"'Tis the great bard Shakespeare himself wrote those words," he answered. "From a play of his called *Mac—*"

"Ah," she broke in, "we Quakers neither read plays, nor do we perform in them. Though some Nantucket folk may, if that way thy persuasion lies."

"Just tell the story!" Josiah growled. "My patience is wearing thin, and my mother's is threadbare as well." He looked over at her, and her smile was a sudden, thin-lipped grimace.

"I agree with my son on substance here, Friend Ishmael," she said in a soft voice, "but not in his particular way of expressing himself."

Josiah was impressed. In her gentle Quaker way, she had made her point, and a solid hit it was, but somehow it landed without wounding their visitor sorely.

"If the captain was a difficult man," the seaman was quick to say, "it was your husband who was the solid bulwark who stood between him and the crew."

"No flattery needed," she remarked. "I knew my husband almost all my life, and was well acquainted with his good points as with the others. He would always do his duty to the letter. I need to hear only the true."

"Then I tell you in all truth, ma'am," Ishmael Black said, if a bit stiffly. "Your husband knew the captain's ill temperament and understood his savage wish for revenge on that certain white whale, though many of us crewman thought it a bogey he had made up. A bogey, that is, until it appeared with the captain's harpoon still stuck in its back, red flags flying."

Josiah could not stand the smugness with which that last had been delivered, and he responded with a sharp, "And I suppose the captain's leg was still embedded in its teeth!"

"Josiah. . ." his mother warned.

Ishmael Black turned and gave Josiah a strange smile. "Well, partly right, lad. Sperm whales *are* the largest toothed whales, 'tis true. But that leg was long gone, like Jonah himself, into the belly of the whale. Churned up and ate up, dissolved for that white devil's dinner a season or more before. You will not unknot this story with such a lack of natural history."

Then, leaving his lesson hanging between them, the seaman turned back to Josiah's mother. "Your good husband, ma'am, understood his job aboard ship was to take care of the crew and to deal with the captain's wishes, difficult though they might be. In this case, not an easy business. And he was respected by almost the entire crew for this."

There was an unease once that had been said.

Josiah's gaze shifted upward so he was staring at the ceiling. On the other hand, he'd seen that his mother's gaze had swiftly looked floorward.

In the deep, deep silence that followed, Josiah wondered what the seaman had meant by "almost." Who didn't respect his father? Was it the captain? Was it some of the sailors? Was it Ishmael Black himself? Or was he speaking of the whale?

When Ishmael made no concession, no quick edit, no explanation, Josiah let his question drift away unasked. But it remained, like a marlinspike, embedded in his gut.

As it was a lovely day, the three of them went outside and sat on two benches under a tree in new bud. As they settled themselves, Josiah took a deep breath of the spring air.

Ishmael Black cleared his throat and loosened the sailor's scarf around his neck before it seemed he was truly ready to tell the final part of his tale.

The hard part, Josiah already knew—the part where his father died. But he schooled himself not to think about it before it had to be told.

"And so, I signed the articles," the seaman was saying. "And while I had some experience on ships, having sailed several times in the merchant service, little of it prepared me for being on a whaler. Or sailing under Captain Ahab, who was unlike any captain I had sailed with before."

Josiah couldn't contain himself. He leaned forward and said, "The one-legged captain, and was he fierce?"

"Fierce," Ishmael Black said, rolling the word around in his mouth. "I was told by one one of the owners that Ahab was 'a swearing good man,' and then that owner added, 'Better to sail with a moody *good* captain than a laughing bad one.'"

Josiah had barely digested that bit of informa-tion when Ishmael Black added smugly, "With that I thought to be satisfied. Little was I or any of the others to know, at least not at first, that a good captain obsessed with thoughts of revenge on a single whale was not to be trusted and would end up losing his masters' money and killing us all."

Josiah stared as his mother put her hand on the top

of the seaman's hand. "Not all, Friend Ishmael," she reminded him. "Not all died. And surely it was not thy fault in this. Those who survive a tragedy often take on its garments as their own."

"There are some who die yet live on," he responded, making a small frown as if to show his apology for still being alive. "For I yet had a job to do."

Josiah thought: *And I know what job he means.*

Ishmael Black took her hand in his. He looked intently into her face. "And I only am escaped alone to tell thee."

For a minute she looked startled and left her hand in his. Then, withdrawing the hand gently, she said: "Book of Job." Adding as if an afterthought, or as a lesson to a child in First Day school, "In the Hebrew Bible."

"Yes, Job said it." Ishmael Black smiled at her, with a face full of charm and a great deal of understanding.

Again, she looked startled but did not contradict him, and simply folded her hands together on her lap.

But Josiah knew that Ishmael was wrong. It was *not* Job who had spoken those words. It was four separate messengers coming to warn Job about his losses at home. That passage was one of his mother's favorites, explaining how God tested all people. After every shipwreck, every ship gone missing, it was part of her witness at Meeting. And now it was her loss to carry forward forever.

For a moment, Josiah wondered why Ishmael Black had changed the speaker of the line. Perhaps to make himself bigger, more important in the story? Or maybe to flatter a rich widow? Though, Josiah knew, she was not rich, except in her house and in her heart. Also, as a good Quaker woman, she was supposed to be immune to flattery. Though it hardly looked that way now. He could feel an anger growing, that darkness Quakers often warned of, rising inside him.

He knew he could not stay there any longer, watching his mother fall under this charlatan's spell. Whistling to his dog, he left the two of them in the middle of the story, his father's death still untold, and ran off down the path to speak to his friends in the town. If there was to be any counsel, he wanted it to come from boys his own age, for they alone would understand the true knot of this problem and offer their own advice.

In his mind's eye, Josiah saw them as a cozy pair, hand in hand still. And it was that false image he would carry with him for quite some time.

CHAPTER FIVE:
Poor Advice

It was indeed a glorious morning, perfect for running, but Josiah felt none of that. He felt instead like the errant child, that annoying boy who was always underfoot and in the way. It was a new feeling. Neither his mother nor father had ever made him feel like that. They were always a trio, a triad, a family. He had been included in everything, been part of every important decision since he was a small boy. But he had friends who had no such closeness, who even disbelieved his account of their family sit-downs, as his father called them.

Zeke barked, as if guessing Josiah's thoughts.

Perhaps, Josiah thought, *perhaps Ishmael Black does not know the parable of the Prodigal Son.* But just as suddenly he wondered which one of them was supposed to be that young man in the story, the reprobate, the one who ran off, the one who was later welcomed back by his grieving father.

That's the problem with parables. They can be read in so many ways!

As his mother often said, "Parables, like any stories, are changed between the mouth and ear, between the teller and the listener. They are lessons *for* life, not *of* life."

Josiah slowed to a walk, nodding. Her bits of wisdom sometimes took years to untangle. This one suddenly hit him with such clarity he sniffed loudly, loud enough to startle the dog.

But then he thought, *Real life can change just as swiftly. Yesterday morning I had a father and mother and knew the charts of my life. Today I am a small boat awash in a very big and very dark sea.*

And with that premonition—or fairy tale—in his head, he headed straight for the town center, where he knew he could always find some of his friends. That was what he needed now. Not a grown-up who disappeared when one wanted them most, or disappointed their own son by holding a stranger's hand.

As the town came into view, he saw a knot of boys down near the harbor. That was what his father had

called them, "a knot." And each time he had added,
"Just be certain that these are the hearty, well-tied
knots, my boy, not the shoddy, hastily looped ones
who will lead thee into trouble."

As he got closer, Josiah saw that this knot didn't
consist of any of his closest friends. These were indeed a bit on the shoddy side. The ones who did not
finish their lessons for school and even skylarked off
on school days to go fishing or talk their way into
taverns.

There was Rayburn, who tended to sass adults, even
their teacher, because his father was the harbormaster,
and as such, an important man in the town.

Next to Rayburn stood Robert, who followed whatever Rayburn said and was also his cousin. There, too,
were the Coffin twins, Abel and David. They mostly
spoke to one another and not to others. And lagging
behind a bit as usual was Peter, whose mother was—
well, she said she was a widow and took in washing. But nobody had ever known her husband. She'd
moved to the town when Peter had still been a baby.
And no husband tagged behind. *Or so said the gossips*,
Josiah thought. And while his mother always told him
not to believe gossips, but look for the answer of his
own heart, he thought the gossips might be right.
Though Peter was the most solid and hardworking
of that particular knot of boys.

Josiah shrugged. He supposed, as his father said, that gossips were just another kind of storyteller, though often erring on the side of cruelty and petty lies.

Besides, Josiah liked Peter, only tolerating the other four. And, more to the point, none of his closer friends were anywhere near the ships.

"Shoddy knots it is," he said in an undertone to Zeke, who followed closely at his heels without a word or a woof about gossips or knots.

They went down to greet the boys, Zeke with pleasure and Josiah suddenly trying to figure out what he could say to them that would not bring him to tears. *Tears are something for old men and young girls*, he thought. *And I am neither.*

But that thought smacked him in the face like a sudden gust slapping a sail. Tears sprang to his eyes. If Ishmael Black was telling the truth, Father would never get to be an old man who told sea stories by the fire long into the night as Grandpa Starbuck used to do. Like all the old sea captains and mates and sailors did.

And just as that that thought unwound its own rope, Josiah saw that the boys had spotted him and were coming over to greet him in a body, so it was too late to turn around.

Quickly, he pulled off his neckerchief and made

loud sneezing noises into it, drying his eyes in the process, then waved the rag at them, saying, "I have caught that springtide sniffle again." Which made them stand back a bit in case it transferred to them as well.

His eyes now dry, he knotted the neckerchief back around his neck and said, "I have news to tell."

News was what men called it. Gossip was what women did. The knot of boys knew him as a mostly silent friend. He rarely had news to share. So, they quickly surrounded him, forgetting about the springtide sniffle, which had already disappeared.

No one was surprised by this move, surely not the boys or any watchers, either. Nantucket was an island. And like all islands, it thrived on local news, being so far from other shores. And thrived even more on close companionships.

Josiah began in the only way he knew how, with the absolute truth. "Today my mother is a widow and I am now a fatherless boy," he said, the words tumbling out so fast the boys leaned in to try and separate them.

As the knot of boys looped closer around him, a whirlpool of their questions bubbled up, a tidal wave needing answers.

"How?"

"Why?"

"Where'd you hear?"

"What makes you know it's true?"

"Does old Peleg know?"

"A white whale? No such thing!"

"Do you believe this intruder?"

A push.

A shove.

A snort.

A laugh.

A slap.

"Stop it!" Josiah hissed. "Of course I do not want to believe it, but I must." He took a quick breath. "At least I think I do."

At the stony authority in his voice, they all fell silent.

That was when he told them everything. Or at least most everything, beginning with the knock on the door, but leaving out his sobbing in the meadow. And for the first time with this particular knot of boys, he had their full and complete attention.

Even Rayburn left off his usual sass.

Without discussing what they had just heard, the six of them walked over to one of the unoccupied wharfs and sat down, their feet swinging out above the low tide.

They sat there for some time, Josiah working his

hardest not to sniffle and ruin their newfound camaraderie, until Rayburn suddenly said, "Let's talk to the harbormaster."

He meant his father, of course, but he always used his father's title as if it conferred a kind of status on Rayburn as well. Which it often did.

"What could *he* do for Josiah?" Peter asked sensibly.

Josiah would have thrown his arm over Peter's shoulder if it wouldn't have likely caused a riot with the boys. It was just the sensible question he was about to ask Rayburn himself.

"The harbormaster," Rayburn began, a bit testily, "knows everything about the ships and their timetables and why they are late. He can find out if this Ishmael fellow actually signed on the *Pequod* and if he stayed the full voyage or was put off onto another ship."

That, Josiah thought, *is the most reasonable thing I have ever heard Rayburn say,* though he would never have voiced such a thing out loud.

The Coffin twins looked at one another and said at almost the same time, "And give fatherly advice."

Robert added, "Or help you ship out on a whaler yourself to—"

"Don't be an ass," Rayburn said, which made whatever else Robert was about to offer dribble away and leave the rest of the conversation beached.

"I'm not sure . . ." Josiah said, but he suddenly realized he *was* sure.

Getting away from the island might be the best thing he *could* do. *Really* clear his head. Spend some time with grown men, not with his mother all day. Especially as she now had a *real* man around the house, a man she seemed to favor. Not a boy tasked to behave like a man.

Yet I have been doing that task well enough till now, he thought bitterly. Though he knew deep down he wasn't ready to ship out on a whaler. Maybe some other kind of ship.

"Yes," he said to Rayburn. "I should like to talk with the harbormaster if he has time for me. Yes, and thank thee."

He rarely used the Quaker *thee* and *thou* with boys his age, but it seemed right to use it now, as he looked gratefully around at them.

But he was also thinking that his father had been wrong about this knot of boys. Not sloppily knotted at all. *And maybe if Father was wrong about them, he could have been wrong about other things, too.*

That was a huge leap for Josiah. He had always idealized his father, a man faithful to his wife and his son, and also to his work onboard whatever ship he sailed.

But . . . Reluctantly, Josiah finished the thought.

Sometimes a man—even a good man—can get something wrong. Perhaps the harbormaster will know.

He nodded at Rayburn, who stood up first, the rest following right after. Then they traipsed behind him in a row, Josiah at his heels, then Robert, the twins, and Peter last, all heading towards the harbormaster's quarters.

The Quarters were up a set of stairs, in a building on the side of the harbor itself. It consisted of three spare rooms: one an office, one a kitchen with a well-equipped pantry, and the third a bunkroom with three beds for quick naps between storms, shipwrecks, drownings, or other disasters.

The harbormaster was not alone. There were three other men with him, all talking at the same time, like a flock of gulls after the same piece of flotsam. Captains they might have been, or owners of ships. Josiah recognized none of them. But they were all nattering and laughing about the difficulty of finding new recruits for their ships.

When the boys went in without knocking, the men glared at them as intruders into their serious business conversations. One man shrugged heavily when the boys gave no excuses for barging in.

The harbormaster quickly gave the aggrieved men a small signal with his hands, to let him have a moment to deal strictly with the unwanted intrusion.

Josiah took this as a good sign. He could offer himself to them as a partial solution to their problems—and his own. So, smiling, he stepped forward and began a stuttering attempt. "Sirs, I . . . I wish . . . I wish to ship out to sea. I have been born to it. My . . . my grandfather was a captain, my . . . my father a first mate . . ."

Two of the men shook their heads dismissively, and the third—a short, stocky man with a small beard—glared and said, "How old art thee, boy? Does thy mother know thee art here?"

Before Josiah could stutter out an answer to this, Rayburn said, "He is my age, sir, and my father knows him. He is Josiah Starbuck and . . ."

The harbormaster put a hand on Josiah's shoulder. "He is a good, smart lad, and a canny sailor. His father is first mate on the *Pequod*, and—"

The bearded man's eyes lit up. "Crazy old Ahab's ship? She's overdue, I hear."

"News travels swiftly in these islands," the harbormaster said in a soothing, considerate voice.

"Aye," another of the men said, who was so old, his wrinkles had wrinkles. "Even faster than old wives' gossip, too, I warrant."

The three men laughed at this, but the boys and the harbormaster were silent, the harbormaster because he was clearly considering his next statement carefully, and the boys because the harbormaster had cautioned them all with an uplifted finger to stay silent.

When the harbormaster spoke again, it was with quiet mastery. "We do not laugh at such things here on the island, not the way you mainlanders do. But Josiah here is the same age as my son, Rayburn." He nodded in Rayburn's direction. "Which means he is too young to sign the Articles on his own. His father is at sea, and his mother—who is clerk of the Nantucket Friends Meeting here—will not, I am certain, *willingly* sign for him. And should she ask me, I would certainly advise her not to let him ship out until his father returns. But she is a woman of faith and honor and much respected in our community and makes her own decisions. She is not to be trifled with, gentlemen, but she knows quite well how to speak truth to power. And you should be minded of it."

"Ah!" said the bearded man, as if that made it all clear. "A Quaker lady, then. We three are Friends as well. With a modest amount of power, and wives who speak their truth to us on a daily basis."

The other men nodded in agreement, trying hard to conceal their smiles, but failing.

The harbormaster turned back to Josiah. "I will not tell your mother about this meeting, Josiah. And if you are as smart as I believe you to be, you will not mention it, either. And now, boys," he said, addressing them all, "leave us *men* to our business."

They knew they were dismissed without any more of a hearing, so silently, they filed outside and down the stairs, where Zeke greeted them joyously—but his joy was not returned.

An easterly wind was singing in their ears. And even when the boys got to the walkway, where they might have made a complaint to one another, none of them spoke. The injustice of the men's conversation and the harbor-master's treatment of him burned in Josiah's chest until he thought he would have to vomit it out.

He did not. But it was close.

Chapter Six:
Changing Winds

As a Quaker, Josiah was used to silent meetings, where no one spoke unless prompted to by that still, quiet voice—the voice of God—urging one to speak. Josiah had never yet spoken out in Meeting himself, but his mother testified powerfully and almost always spoke to his personal condition, something he had been wrestling with, though he had not spoken to her about it at all. But those were held indoors and sitting on hard wooden benches. This silence between the boys was a different kind of silence, with no hope from a word of God in his ear.

He shook his head vigorously, then turned to Rayburn. "I need to sail, to clear my head. To think about . . ." He couldn't, wouldn't say it again.

They all knew what he meant and nodded.

"I could go with you," Peter offered.

Rayburn said, "Have you checked the weather?"

As one they looked toward the south where the wind was now rising a bit. These were all boys with boats. They knew wind and waves. It was the first thing they thought about when the word "sail" was mentioned, the last thing they heard before falling asleep.

"I won't be long," Josiah said. "And Zeke will come with me."

The dog looked up at his name, ears raised, then down at the ground as if admitting that going on Josiah's little catboat was *not* something he wanted to do. After all, boats trembled, shook, bounced. They could not be counted on to stay afloat, and neither could a dog.

Zeke was decidedly *not* a water dog. He liked firm ground beneath his feet and preferred to stay out of the wind. A hearth fire was where he belonged, with a bowl of meat nearby. Knowing that boys paid no attention to what a dog wanted, he gave a resigned *woof* and looked north. Then he sniffed and walked over to stand as close to his boy as he could without actually climbing into Josiah's trousers.

The boys all nodded, except for Abel, who shrugged, and then the knot turned to go back to the big wharf to watch Josiah's sailing form from there.

―――――――

Josiah whistled for Zeke to follow him down to the small end of the harbor, where his little catboat *Petrel* was snugged up on the stark Nantucket sand.

He could have asked for help from the boys, and it would have halved the time it actually took him to get the boat into the water. But this was *his* problem, *his* anger, and *his* penance to perform. He didn't want to talk any more to them. *The only head that needs clearing,* he thought, *is my own.*

He untied *Petrel*'s painter from the large post that had held her safe from any extra high tides, and then pulled her around, stern first till at last the small waves lapped at her side.

The catboat's mast sat well forward in the bow and, once the sail was pulled tight, resembled a petrel's wing, which was what had given him the idea for her name. He yanked *Petrel* down the beach towards the waterline until the little waves lapped at her prow. Zeke slunk along behind, miserable, but his boy did not turn to check on him.

Josiah's father had *Petrel* built for Josiah's twelfth birthday, and that gave them time for three dozen lessons on her before his father had sailed off as first mate on the *Pequod*, knowing he would probably not be back for Josiah's thirteenth birthday.

"And possibly," as his father had added to Josiah, "not for thy next birthday, either." They both knew that what was really important was his fifteenth birthday—that was when Nantucket boys usually proclaimed themselves men, deciding on going further in school, or apprenticing to a tradesman, or signing on one of the big ships as a sailor.

"Will thee be back for my fifteenth birthday?" Josiah had asked his father, who had given the expected answer: "Whaling trips take as long as they take."

That wasn't a new notion to Josiah. Every child on Nantucket whose father was a whaler had that conversation. They knew it in their bones before it was ever spoken.

It takes as long as it takes.

As long as there are whales.

As long as the rich whale oil flows.

As long as the captain says.

As long as God allows.

Even to eternity, Josiah thought, but would not let tears fill his eyes this time. *Even to eternity.*

Hefting Ezekiel into the stern, Josiah took off his shoes and stockings, pushing the stockings down deep into each shoe, and leaving them close to the dog. "Guard!" he said.

Even though Zeke hated the rocking motion of the boat, he lay down on the uncomfortable shoes, as if guarding them with his life would make him safe from the brutal sea.

Then Josiah bent over and rolled his pants legs up till his calves and knees were bare, and pushed the little boat farther out, till it drifted free of the sand. Only then did he scramble over the port side, which was nearer to the shore.

During that inelegant scramble—with the boys hooting from the shore—Josiah's sheath came undone from the belt, falling to the bottom of the catboat. He let it nestle there, next to Zeke's nose, knowing it would be safe till he could fix it back on his belt.

He ignored his friends' jeers.

Josiah was proud of the fact that his pants stayed dry. That had been one of his first lessons. He had learned it, and all the other lessons, well.

"Thank thee, Father," he whispered into the wind.

Sailing with wet clothes was not just uncomfortable, but could be dangerous to a sailor's health. That's why one took rain gear along. But as he wasn't planning to go far or for long, just for a bit of head-clearing, his lack of rain gear was not a problem, this time.

Yes, the sky was darkening a bit, but the wind was still mostly from the south. Well, southeasterly. There were no heavy, dark, rounded clouds in the sky. So, he wasn't really worried about a storm, though they could blow up suddenly this time of year. But to be safe, he would just go out for a bit and then sail right back. Enough for head-clearing. No more.

He was glad his father hadn't been around for this his hasty, inelegant scramble into *Petrel,* or his stammering attempt with the old seamen to get a berth on one of their ships. Thinking of the latter, he was suddenly ashamed of having tried. And as quickly as he had that thought, his eyes filled, because his father would never again be around again to lend his support or take Josiah to task.

Ever.

Using the old single oar, he paddled *Petrel* farther out into the harbor, all the while checking the wind, which was still blowing steadily from the southeast.

Yes, he was angry, upset, even seething a bit, but he was too much of a sailor to risk a bad blow. He would only go for an hour and then come back. An hour out, maybe two coming back if the wind turned. By then his head should have cleared. And maybe by the time he got back, Ishmael Black might have cleared out, too.

At last Josiah began to raise the sail. And didn't it belly out nicely, the little catboat picking up speed. Not too fast, but not as soft, as slow as before. He was on a reach now. Good old *Petrel,* she was a safe boat. A happy boat.

But there *was* a bit more wind than he'd expected. Still, that sail was a strong one. It had been his father's sail on *his* first catboat, and made of quality canvas,

outlasting the old boat itself. With good care, his father had often told him, that sail was not likely to
deteriorate from sun and rain, as long as it was well
looked after.

As long as it is well looked after. Josiah would not forget
that.

Then he lowered the center board, took the tiller in
hand, and set course to take them out of the harbor
and along the coast for the much-needed head-
clearing.

There was a small shudder as the wind turned
slightly, and the boat keeled over a bit. He shifted his
weight towards the windward side to be sure to keep
the boat reasonably flat, and the boat righted itself.

It is, he thought again, *a sweet little boat.* Carvel-
planked with cedar, on oak frames. Father had spent a
good penny on her.

Josiah gave a half smile. It was often said in Nantucket that Quakers rarely spent more than needed.
Indeed, there was an old Nantucket proverb that the
only ones who could buy from a Yankee and still
make a profit was a Quaker!

Probably Father spent more than he wished, Josiah
thought, *because I am his only child, his only son. Only one
he will ever have now.* His parents had lost twin sons at
birth, four years before him. *Twins.* He often wondered
what it would have been like, growing up with two

older brothers. They would have been eighteen this next month. Probably would have shipped out on the *Pequod* with their father.

"Only survivor . . ." Ishmael had said. And that would have meant the twins would be dead now as well. If they had lived. Josiah shook his head again, and bit his lip slightly. *These thoughts are not helping.*

Josiah soon got *Petrel* directly on course, though she still had the collywobbles from that bit of unexpected wind. *Collywobbles!* The word made him smile. *Collywobbles!* was something his mother liked to say when anything—a boat, a sail, a boy's stomach, a seaman's head, or a dog—were shaky for a while.

He wondered briefly how she was doing, then shook his head. It was his father he should be thinking about. And yet he had to put his family firmly out of mind now and concentrate on the boat.

As he did so, he could feel his head truly beginning to clear, even as the wind rose more. Not to a shriek—that would be a disaster—but to a steady wind, which made the Nantucket coastline scoot by.

Below the sound of the rising wind, Josiah just managed to hear another sound, a scrabbling whine coming from behind his feet. Or maybe he was just aware of the reverberations through his bare toes. He looked down just as Zeke managed to push away from the shoes he has been guarding, glance around, and shake himself thoroughly.

But before Josiah could guess what the frightened dog might do next, Zeke was already halfway over the port side of the boat, and ready to swim to the safety of the quickly disappearing shore.

"Ezekiel!" Josiah cried out, dropping his hold on the tiller and reaching desperately for the dog's haunches with both hands.

But Zeke was gone over the port side with an incautious splash, first into, then under a small-capped wave.

Josiah turned back, needing to deal with both the sail and the tiller. He pushed his shoes and stockings, plus the sheathed knife/marlinspike, into the space beneath his tiller seat for safety.

"Be that way!" he muttered. "Stupid dog!"

But half a minute later, having gotten hold again of the boat's progress, Josiah turned, squinting to see if the dog had made it yet to shore.

Zeke was a competent swimmer in a quiet pool, a puddle romper, but this was a swift tide and heading into a deep channel and from there to the ocean. It was not for any kind of dog. Especially one who hated sea water.

There was no sign of Zeke nearing the sand, no grumpy dog shaking himself dry, shaking to remove his own collywobbles.

No sign at all.

"Zeke?" Josiah called.

Silence.

He bent over the port side. "Ezekiel?"

He feared his voice would be lost in a sudden rise of the wind, but tried again: "EZEKIEL!"

And again, his voice hoarse with fear: "EZEKIEL!"

Glancing desperately over the starboard side, he saw a bobbing head, not moving toward shore at all. Zeke must have been dragged under the boat's shallow bottom by the rushing water, and while he had managed to come up again, he was now scrabbling with frantic paws to catch up with *Petrel*, which—with each gust of wind puffing the sail—was leaving him farther behind.

"*Stupid* dog!" Josiah cried out, not in anger this time, but in terror. He yanked on the tiller, coming about sharply, to bring the boat into the wind. "In irons," Father called it.

And all the while, knowing the danger, knowing that he might not be able to sail fast enough *into* the wind, that he might damage the sail, even frantic that he might be too late to save his dog, or that *Petrel* itself might be swamped, and that he as well as Zeke might have to swim for their lives, Josiah turned to battle the wind and the sea for his dog's sake.

And for his own.

CHAPTER SEVEN:
Running Before the Wind

*P*etrel was already taking on water, partly from the rain that had begun to fall from the darkening sky, and partly because the sudden turn into the wind had made the catboat dip down on its starboard side, causing a wave to swamp over the gunwale.

Josiah had no time to bail now, only time to maneuver the boat close enough to the frantically paddling dog, trying to line up next to him.

Josiah thought that did little to offer Zeke confidence, as it probably looked to him like a formidable wooden wall to climb. But as Josiah bent over the side, endangering both the boat and himself in his effort to save the dog, Zeke opened his mouth to bark joyously and was slapped with a mouthful of salt water. He spit quite a bit out, all at once.

Still, that might have been enough to sink him, had Josiah not reached out in one last heroic effort, grabbing the shaggy ruff around Zeke's neck with both hands, and hauling him—by wish and by prayer—over the side of the boat to safety.

Zeke rewarded him by throwing up heartily on Josiah's bare feet.

"Thank thee, Ezekiel!" Josiah said to the dog. "'Tis lucky there is already enough water in the bottom of the boat to wash this vomit away."

He meant it part in exasperation, part as a joke, but it sounded like both fear and relief.

Either Zeke did not hear, or was still too frightened to do anything but pull himself forward miserably on his belly toward the cuddy, the enclosed space that must have looked a lot to him like a small, safe cave at the boat's prow. There he curled into a ball and would not come out, no matter how much Josiah called his name.

Josiah knew that the amount of water in a boat as small as *Petrel* was could quickly make it unstable. So, holding the tiller in one hand and grabbing the bailing pail in the other, he began to frantically bail out as much of the water as he could, while at the same time, he worked on turning the boat's prow out of the wind.

It meant they would be sailing away from Nantucket harbor, not toward it, which was what he truly wanted to do. Get back, pull *Petrel* up onto the sand, and race up the hill to home.

He was now more than ready to confront Ishmael Black. Ask his intentions. Hear the real story of what happened to his father, not be sluffed off by a *that is all I saw as I swam away* fairy tale. Give his mother a hug. Change into dry clothes. Sit down for tea.

But there was no gain in trying to sail back into the wind, which had already gone from a strong southeasterly into an unforeseen and dangerous nor'easter.

The little boat was shuddering from the wind's impact. And he himself was beginning to shudder as well from the sudden cold. Great sailing ships like the *Pequod* might be able to sail back into the wind safely, but not a catboat. Not *Petrel*.

She was an inshore boat, made for day-sailing in moderate conditions. The water and wind were well past that now. He knew *Petrel* did not have the heft to handle them. If he wasn't careful, she would founder and capsize, and that would be the end of one small boat, one small boy, and one small dog.

His only chance now was reducing sail by "scandalizing," and running before the wind, heading west with the wind at his back, then finding a small harbor as soon as possible, and putting in there to wait out the storm or to walk the long, wet way home from whatever part of Nantucket they'd landed in.

Good reasoning, son. The words were all but lost in the wind, but Josiah heard them. His father's words.

He did not question them.

Of course, the danger was that the wind was no longer a soft kitten toying with his sail but now a tiger at his back. It might push him into the vast domain of the brutal ocean if he wasn't careful enough with sheet and tiller. *Petrel* might actually capsize if he was not alert . . . if he was stupid.

The ocean that has already killed thee, Father, he thought. *Mother could not stand having us both gone. Not so soon, one after the other.*

Though of course many island women had stood just that. The sea, even in Nantucket Harbor, could be a harsh master. That was drummed into every boy, every girl on the island.

Yes, he told himself, *or I may have to go all the way to the tip of Nantucket, this wind is so fierce, and that turn at the island's end is going to be a very tricky bit of maneuvering.* He would need all his wits about him to accomplish such a jibe with this wind. Else he risked passing the end of Nantucket and heading out toward the Vineyard, a long way off in the gathering dark. Hours away.

Josiah hoped he really was the canny sailor the harbormaster had called him. Otherwise, it could very well mean *Petrel* being pushed into the vast Atlantic, or fetching up on some truly frightening shoals or rocks of some unknown, unrecorded island shore. Neither of them was a good idea in a catboat.

Neither of them is a good idea in a catboat in a storm, came his father's voice. Or maybe Josiah had just thought of it himself. He didn't dare lose his wits now. At the rate this wind was blowing up, pushing them forward, he was pretty sure—if he kept his wits about him—they could make it to the turn before the dark drew in entirely. If he was granted luck. If he was granted Light.

Oh, Mother, he thought frantically, *help me find the Light. If anyone knows how to find it, it would be thee.*

Josiah was close in his estimation. The little catboat had sped forward as if being chased by a pride of lions. *Sea lions!* It was a very small joke, but any amusement under the circumstances helped.

The canvas sail was so fat-bellied at this point, the wind so fierce, and he so slow scandalizing it, she could be a woman in the last stages of giving birth. Something he had heard about, though of course never witnessed.

Petrel continued going so fast in the closing dark, the wind whistling around the boat, he lost any idea of time.

The rain was still heavy. The only thing Josiah had to concentrate on was keeping *Petrel* steady, and at the same time continuing to bail. He was barely aware of what flashed by on the port side, except to keep *Petrel* far enough from the shoreline that she wouldn't be forced onto any shoals, those hidden rocks that could break his little boat to pieces.

He had not come out with a chart that could have warned him about shoals. And he had little experience this far along the Nantucket coast. None in the dark. All he could do was watch—and pray.

Eye on those demmed rocks, his father whispered in his ear as the last of Nantucket's coast came into partial view.

Soaked from the storm, and with the ocean slopping into the little boat, Josiah was shaking with cold. But still, he was pretty certain—even though he had to strain to see through the rain—that it was, indeed, the end of the island. He and his friends had slept a night on that shore once, though he had not been on his own boat then.

Almost there, he promised himself, and let hope enter his heart.

He had to jibe the boat from its broad reach on starboard tack, the wind pretty much steadily coming over the right rear corner of his boat now. But that was a trick his father had taught him long ago, and he guessed it would serve him well now.

One hand on the tiller, he dropped the bailer and put the other on the sheet, then began the turn that would take *Petrel* into what he remembered of the small harbor. It was already too dark to actually see it.

He was mostly through and out of the worst of the wind when his father shouted in his ear: '*Ware, son! Beware!*

Before he could shake his head to rid it of his father's scold, he heard another sound, an uncanny *whisht* above him. Looking up, he saw that the bottom few yards of sail had torn in two, and both now flapped uselessly in the wind, though the upper part of the sail still held.

Holding for now, he thought, and instinctively stood, trying to catch the two pieces.

That was when he heard a second sound, an even more ominous *creak*.

It took him a frantic two or three seconds to identify the noise, and by then it was too late. The heavy wooden boom, having lost some of the burden of sail, was swinging swiftly toward him. He ducked, but not fast or far enough, and the boom slammed into the side of his head.

His last coherent thought was: *This is the true danger now*. He didn't need his father's voice to warn him.

He tried to keep his balance, but the pain of the

strike to his head so stunned him, he slipped down into the bottom of *Petrel* that was almost, but not quite, emptied of standing water. Then, like his dog, he vomited into the boat.

It may have been mere moments, or possible hours, before Josiah was able to sit up again. He had no way of knowing, except that it was now fully dark.

The wind was screaming over *Petrel*, and his head felt as if it was ringing out the Congregational church's hourly chimes. It got to fourteen bells before he stopped counting.

Sitting up gingerly, he felt a sudden slurp on the only part of his head that didn't hurt. Turning toward the sound, he found himself face-to-face with Zeke, who must have crawled out from somewhere. Josiah had no real memory of rescuing the dog earlier. Just a half picture in his mind of Zeke desperately swimming in the sea.

"Where are we, boy?" he croaked in a voice that was unfamiliar to both of them. Then he looked to port side and realized they were close to some shore. Possibly too close.

He did not immediately recognize where they were. The dark disguised much of it. All he knew was that it didn't look like Nantucket. Or at least nothing seemed familiar.

Of course, he reminded himself, *it is hard to make out much because the boat is now shuddering, battling the wind, and because of the rain, and because it is nearly total dark, and because . . .*

Mostly because he had a sudden searing and unexplainable pain in his head that hammered at his temples. It made his eyes seep. He swiped his arm across his face, and the wet sleeve of his jacket only made things worse.

He peered out again at the shore.

Could it be one of the small islands at the tip of Nantucket? Could it be the Vineyard? That was the only big island west and north of Nantucket. He hadn't sailed there enough to be sure, and never at night. Had he missed the actual turn while he was felled by the boom?

Am I actually awake?

He sat back on the little bench at the stern, shook out his cramped hand for a second, then put it back on the tiller.

But suddenly both tiller and hand shook so much, they made his head hurt all over again.

Thee has to make land, son, his father's voice said. *I judge the winds to be . . .*

"Forty-five degrees," Josiah said aloud.

Good boy.

Josiah knew his father wasn't really there. He also knew the wind was at the height where he could just about still sail *Petrel*. *But a few degrees more wind,* he thought, *even if I could still manage to reef the torn sail,* Petrel *is likely to capsize. I have to make landfall soon or . . .* There were no more *ors* left. He didn't need his dead father to tell him that.

Good boy.

The voice was quieter, almost whispering. Or the wind was louder. Josiah knew that with no food, no shelter, no charts, no compass, no rain gear, no coats or blanket, no dry clothing, there was nothing left except hope. And his mother's belief in the Light that guided.

His own beliefs had faltered somewhere back when the boom hit his head. There was no way he could see the Light now. Or hear the small, still voice.

Unless . . . Unless that really *had* been his father's voice. Josiah strained to hear more. But the only sounds were the wind, the rain, and the church bells. And he knew only the wind and rain were real. The bells weren't.

He felt bad about himself, but worse for Zeke. He should have left his dog behind.

Land, his father's voice said again, spectral, fading.

"But *what* land, Father?" Josiah asked the dark.

There was no answer of course. His father—his real father—was dead.

Josiah knew he had been speaking to himself. And himself didn't know the answer.

The wind dropped a bit. Josiah could feel it on his face now, could hear its particular voice. He suddenly remembered that sound.

Petrel *must have come around the Nantucket northern coast so quickly, I didn't notice,* he thought. *It is either a curse or a miracle.*

No miracles on the sea, his father's voice said sadly, a valediction.

Angrily, Josiah called out, "Then what about Ishmael Black?"

Or a mighty blow, his father added, not specifying whether he meant the wind or the boom, the whale, or Ishmael's miraculous ride home.

This time, Josiah ignored the voice.

The only sane thing would be to find a small beach, pull the boat up on shore, and shelter under her. And then in the morning—the Lord willing, and the nor'easter passed—he could figure out where they had landed. Then he could sew up the sail, and he and Zeke and *Petrel* could limp their way back down till they reached Nantucket's other end and sail to the harbor with a grand story and a bit of Nantucket glory to share.

Plus Nantucket history to make—both gossip and news.

Presuming, of course, this was still Nantucket, presuming they were still alive, presuming it wasn't all a dream from the blow to his head.

Don't be presumptuous, boy, his father said. *Listen to thy head, not thy heart.*

But all Josiah's head said was pain-pain-pain.

All his heart said was fear-fear.

His hand on the tiller, he made another hard turn at the end of the land and tacked as best he could down the coast till it was too dark and dangerous to go any farther.

The dog settled so close to him he could hear Zeke's heart beating faster than his own. He bent over for a second to pet Zeke, to calm him, and the boat leaped up as if harpooned, then grounded itself on a layer of hidden rocks and sand.

Bad landing, Josiah thought bitterly, trying without hope to gain control of the boat. His last thought— before he and the dog were catapulted out of the boat onto the treacherous shore—was that Father had been right as always. In the dark, in the muddle of his head, he had forgotten to keep an eye on those demmed rocks.

He could have whined like a child that it had not been his fault. It was too dark. And raining.

But it *had* been his fault, the whole sorry mess. Doing anything about it would have to wait until it was light. If he and Zeke lasted until then.

With that thought, he passed out, his head facing forward but still in danger from the turn of the tide.

CHAPTER EIGHT:
The Big One

Z eke hit the rocks as well, but was quick enough to
scrunch into a ball and roll into the water, which
pushed him onto the sandy part of a small island's
shore. He would have scampered up out of the water
entirely, but the sound of Josiah's moaning made him
stop, then turn back into the scary tide.

It was less courage than the sound of his boy in
pain, the one who fed him, who petted him, who cud-
dled next to him when lightning made its awful crack-
ing sounds. The boy who recently had plucked him
from the sea.

He grabbed the boy's collar and, with more love and
determination than wit, dragged him out of the water
and onto the compromised shore.

Then Zeke sat on his hind legs and howled, a sound
so desperate Josiah's eyes fluttered open.

"What . . . ?" Josiah began, then coughed out what felt like a pint of salt water that had been poisoning his stomach.

"Where?" he asked, certainly a more reasonable question. But it was still dark, and his head ached, so he had no answer for that question, either. He just knew instinctively to crawl towards higher ground. Higher, yes, though still awfully wet, but at least it was no longer rocky, and he was away from the powerful waves that kept on flinging themselves against the shoals as if trying to grab him by the ankles and claim him back.

At last, high enough, or so he hoped, to make it through until morning, Josiah sank down into the sodden grass in another kind of swoon with Zeke snuggled up by his side.

They slept a restless hour, and after Zeke got up to relieve himself, a further four hours, curled around one another for warmth until a weak sun peeked up over the eastern horizon.

Zeke woke first, shook himself dry, stretched a bit, then went to lift his leg against a plank from the catboat. The plank had been flung up onto the sand and stuck there upright, an invitation for any dog, though he had missed seeing it in the violence and dark of their landing.

Afterwards, Zeke ignored the noisy early morning birds overhead, returning directly to Josiah, licking his boy's face until Josiah swatted at him without ever connecting.

But at least that made Josiah sit up and look around, grunting, "Still alive, then." It had not been a given.

Though it was not yet fully dawn, Josiah could make out three things: two on the shore, and one behind him, out of the water's way. On the shore were two pieces of his boat. Probably planks from *Petrel*'s bottom. One was somehow standing erect in the sand. The other was lying flat on the beach.

The bulk of the catboat—at least seen from that distance—seemed intact, half in and half out of the water. But her mast and sail were scattered upon the rocks.

He thought he remembered something happening to the sail, but wasn't certain what or how. He didn't remember reaching this part of Nantucket, or wherever he was. That whole time was a blank. His last memory was of being on the sea.

"Have to get back home," he told himself, his voice sounding weak and uncertain. "Have to tell Mother . . ."

Mother. There was something about his mother. . . . She was in some kind of danger, he thought, though he couldn't quite remember what. Or perhaps it was his father. Josiah's mind seemed full of fog.

But he would be going nowhere until he checked the actual damage to his boat, of that much he was certain. And if the boat was beyond repair—well, it would be a long walk back to the part of Nantucket where he lived. Of that he was also certain. Maybe a full day or more.

But first, he thought, *first I have to get my head working again. Might have hit it on the rocks.* It felt as if it was ticking like Mother's grandfather clock. *Tick-tock, tick-tock.* Each sound sent shock waves through his body.

When he tried to stand, it wasn't just the head that hurt. His entire body was too shaky to let him get up. Sitting seemed to be the better option.

So, sitting, he swiveled around to look inward at the land itself. The two things that he could vaguely make out were some kind of fisherman's shack atop a near-by hill, which seemed close enough walk to, at least when he was ready to stand and move. And behind the shack—quite a long way behind, actually—a larger structure like . . . like . . .

He squinched his eyes, trying to see it better. But the structure had begun to shimmer in the rays of the rising sun, and he couldn't quite figure it out.

An arch of some kind? A church arch?

Sudden hope sprang up in his chest. Where there was a church, there would be people. People who would help him get home. And suddenly he remembered hearing bells, right before . . . before the time he couldn't recall. Maybe those had been church bells after all.

He brushed his still-damp right sleeve across his eyes, which didn't actually help. Now the shimmer had become something more like mist.

Or is it the skeleton of a church arch? That would mean no people after all.

He tried to remember if there was a church, an old deserted church, on the end of Nantucket, which now seemed unlikely. He tried to remember the charts he had studied when sailing with his father around their island, since he had no chart at hand. But for some reason he did not want to think about his father because it made his head hurt even more, but in a different way. Instead, he lay down once again, falling quickly into another sleep.

Zeke sniffed at the comatose boy from head to toe, as carefully as any doctor with a patient, then curled around him again. But as he lay there, he bristled with readiness. His boy was not to be disturbed.

When Josiah awoke, the sun was right overhead. He felt a bit better, a bit warmer, no longer wet, but covered with sand fleas, plus he had a hunger that wouldn't go away.

"When did I last eat?" he wondered aloud. He simply could not remember.

"First things first," he whispered to himself, sitting up with great care, like some old man needing a nurse.

He was no longer dizzy. *That* was a relief!

Getting slowly to his knees, he still felt a bit wobbly, but not dizzy. Then, one leg at a time, he managed to stand upright.

He felt a liberation from that strange sleep, and from the fog he partially recalled. Brushing himself off, he stretched. Nothing felt broken, only aching. He took account of each limb.

He didn't feel totally himself, but he felt that he could still figure out his next steps without falling over, without needing more sleep.

"Decisions," Josiah said, loud enough to startle the dog, who ran over to his side. "First, I have to decide if the boat is fixable." Though for the life of him, he couldn't remember what had happened to the boat.

Zeke danced around him as if understanding what his boy was saying.

"And the mast and the sail . . ." There was something about the mast and sail that still nagged at him. But he couldn't fish it up. He knew the answer was down on the shoal, but he was strangely reluctant to go there, knowing only that something bad had happened to the boat and to him on that rocky shore. The thought of it, the mystery of it, filled him with a kind of dread.

But he also knew that the tide was soon to turn, and he had to get down there and bring *Petrel* up onto the sands. And even farther. Up onto the grassy part of the island, else possibly he would lose her forever.

So, without further conversation with himself, he turned away from the sight of the shack and the strange arch, and walked a bit stiff-legged down to the wreckage of his boat.

It took barely a couple of minutes to get there, and already the tide was pulling at *Petrel*'s stern, trying to loosen her hold on the rocks. There was going to be a tug-of-war, but Josiah was ready for it. If only he didn't lose his footing. If only his head didn't start aching again.

Footing! For the first time he realized he was barefoot. He couldn't remember taking off his shoes or losing them. Perhaps they were still in the boat.

But he had walked barefoot on New England seashores all his life. It would be no problem if he had to do it again.

Besides, it was no use looking for the shoes now. The tide had its own timetable. Boat first. Shoes after.

Wading in carefully, he grabbed *Petrel*'s prow and began to struggle against the obstinate tide that wanted to take her back into the sea.

The hard pulling was making his head hurt even more. And there were those bells again. And half memories of wind, rain. And speaking to his father, though he had no memory of when and where that had been. Or what his father had to say.

But at last, with Zeke's enthusiastic barking urging him on, Josiah managed to pull the catboat—or what was left of her—up onto the shore.

Luckily the oar was still there, too big to float through either of the holes left by the missing two planks. And the bailer.

He saw a bit farther along the small coastline the mast and tattered sail, and the boom were floating, almost free of the rocks. He wasn't certain he could rescue them all, but he had to try.

Like most Nantucket boys, he loved to sail, but didn't like getting into the water. But unlike a lot of his friends, he knew how to swim. It was not the gracious strokes that his mother had taught him, but they were at least coordinated and usually quite strong. Though he felt anything but strong now.

Still, he managed to swim far enough out to grab

the mast, sail, and boom. Then half swimming, half riding on them while kicking with his legs, he got the tattered remnants up onto the rocks, and then onto the sand, before sitting down abruptly and once more falling into a kind of stupor.

It was least an hour later, according to the sun, when Josiah woke to the dog's frantic barking.

Sitting up quickly, a bit dizzily, he saw what looked like the stern of a giant sailing ship passing by in the main channel and heading for open waters.

It was too far out for anyone aboard to have spotted one lonely boy washed up on the end of the big island or the pieces of his boat spread out upon the shore, even if they had been looking for him.

But when he blinked to clear his eyes, the ship disappeared, and he knew it had never been there at all. The dog was now growling, looking down into the ocean, probably at some creature in the sea.

"It's all right, Zeke," he said, putting his arms around the dog's neck, though he knew it wasn't right at all. "Invisible ships can't rescue us, and invisible sea creatures can't get to us on the shore. But if a real ship comes by—if this is even a deep enough channel for them—we will have to be prepared to signal them."

Of course, he knew there might never be a real boat. Or a next time. He and the dog might both still be asleep. Or dead of hunger, of cold, of injuries, or loneliness.

He stopped himself from that dangerous kind of thinking. Today was just beginning, and someone might notice he was gone and send out a search party. Maybe the harbormaster and the boys. Maybe his mother. Even that Ishmael Black.

Ishmael. Josiah suddenly remembered. Anger blossomed in him again.

It made his head hurt.

But he could not count on other people to find him. And right now, he had something else to do.

"'Tis time to see what that shack holds," he told Zeke, who had already forgotten the passing ship and the water beast and was now dancing around Josiah like a lunatic as they headed inland, like soldiers reconnoitering on foreign soil.

"And that arch," Josiah added, but under his breath, as if half afraid of what they might find there.

Zeke heard the mutter but raced ahead, unconcerned.

Poor Petrel, Josiah thought as he walked on. *More like a wingless bird right now.* But he had worked on the boat often enough with his father. Surely he could fix her enough to sail home.

And with that promising thought, he and Zeke began to climb the small hill to the shack where, if they were lucky, Josiah would find the tools he needed to do a proper job. And possibly, should the shack prove big enough, a place for the two of them to sleep out of the wind and rain.

Chapter Nine:
Shack and Arch

The shack, which perched rather precariously atop the hill, was more of a disappointment than Josiah had feared. If he had hoped for a place to sleep out of the rain, the shack was not long enough or wide enough for a fourteen-year-old boy. Even one on the small side. Both his legs and the dog's would have surely been outside in any storm.

"Better to sleep under *Petrel*," he told Zeke. "Even with her two missing boards."

The shack was tightly closed up with a heavy gray padlock.

There was no key anywhere in sight. If he had hoped to find food or supplies, or a raincoat or a fisherman's boots (even if old); if he'd counted on fish tackle, nets, or lucifers, he would first have to break into the shack, as he had no key to open it with care.

He tried two half-hearted attempts at jerking the door open. *Perhaps the lock is a sham,* he thought. But even though the shack looked frail, it did not give an inch. He kicked at it and only ended up bruising his left foot.

Finally, he reached for his knife or marlinspike to pick the lock and found, to his dismay, that the sheath and all were missing, and he hadn't noticed or even thought about them till now. *Must have disappeared during the mishaps of the previous day and night,* he thought miserably. He had known the sheath's hanger was in bad shape, but not enough to fall off his old belt without him noticing. Except . . . except he had hit his head. Possibly twice. So maybe he *had* noticed and forgot.

So, now it was even more imperative for him to get into the shack and see if there was something he could use for repairing his boat, for fishing so they could eat, anything for keeping the two of them warm if they had to walk the long island to home.

He waited to hear from his father, but that ghost was gone, perhaps forever, having done its job getting Josiah to the island safely. "Though thee might have managed that with a bit more grace," Josiah said aloud to his father. *A father,* he reminded himself, *who is dead,* and he began mourning the loss all over again. "Now I am truly on my own." He said that last even louder, as if to emphasize it, to Zeke, to himself, to his father's ghost.

His father was silent. Zeke licked his hand. Josiah nodded. "You're right—the *two* of us are on our own."

Then he aimed some choice swear words at the shack and its owner, which, as a good Quaker lad, he had only heard some old fishermen use. He had no idea what the words meant, but they were fierce. And he'd never before mouthed such things out loud. He startled both Zeke and himself with the vehemence of his anger, even though it was not at all unusual for a fisherman to put his tackle under lock and key.

"Maybe use a rock?" he mused aloud, before worrying about the actual act of stealing. Every *Thou Shalt Not* in the Bible rose before him, with large, godlike fingers shaking in his direction.

He thought briefly about leaving a note, but he had no paper, nor ink, nor for that matter, a pen. He shrugged. Something to worry about once he was home. Mother would know what to do.

But how could he ever again ask his mother for help? She was the very reason he was stuck here on the tip of Nantucket.

He flushed, thinking about that, the shame of her inviting that stranger into the house. Feeding him. Listening to him. Yet, at the same time, he admonished himself, those were Quaker standbys: *Feed the tired stranger, listen to the lost.*

He turned suddenly to the dog. "We don't need this shack," he said. "Let's go look at that arch!"

Zeke, who had been sniffing around the outside of the shack, barked, and at that moment, Josiah realized that the shack looked just like a coffin standing upright, and made him think once more of Call-Me-Ishmael, riding the coffin to safety. If that was what the seaman actually did.

"Maybe I could push the shack down the hill to the water," Josiah said to Zeke. "And then thee and I could climb aboard and float home." But even as he said it, he knew that would be more dangerous than staying put and waiting for a passing boat. "Probably fatal," he added. The word "fatal" sat like an open wound between them.

The look that Zeke gave him was unreadable.

Josiah was already turned away and staring at the arch. Or rather, staring past it. From this elevation, he could see what he had not seen before. There was water on all sides of the hill on which he stood.

He turned slowly and then looked back to where his boat huddled on the shore. There was water all around.

No denying it now. This was not Nantucket, nor was his big island anywhere close that he could see.

He and the dog and *Petrel* were sitting on a drop of land maybe half a mile around, with nothing close enough to walk to or swim to. He had no idea how far *Petrel* had sailed on her own after he was hit on the head with the boom.

"The boom!" he blurted aloud. As he said it, he remembered the sound, the crack, the pain as it slammed into his head.

The only way they were going to make it home was to fix his boat and sail home.

He started down the hill, not back toward *Petrel*, but forward to the arch. He had to know every inch of this forsaken place. This no-man's-land. Without even a small *woof* of regret, Zeke followed.

The arch was farther away than Josiah had guessed, as if it was receding even as they walked toward it. As they got closer, what had seemed to be a reasonably sized church arch suddenly began to look like a great cathedral arch. Only it was not made of stone, like an ordinary church building, but of something shining, like a jewel.

As they got closer still, Josiah realized his mistake. It was not a bejeweled archway, but one made of bone. And not just any bone. A whale's jawbone.

The jawbone arch reigned over the far side of the island all alone—except for a single small tree that had been twisted into odd, almost beautiful shapes by the prevailing winds and some scrubby bushes down by the waterside that might carry berries later in the season.

Josiah had no idea if the jawbone had come from a beached whale or a hunted whale; whether it had been stripped clean of its shield of skin and internal parts by the wind, by the sea, by birds or men, or by the hand of God himself. He couldn't tell if it was an old arch of bone or new. He could only see that it was huge.

Leviathan was what the whale was called in the old Hebrew Testament. The beast. The one that had devoured Jonah.

Like all Nantucket boys, Josiah knew that most of the Atlantic whales had been wiped out for their blubber and oil. Whalers like his father and whaling ships like the *Pequod* now had to hunt in the Pacific, that other ocean far from tidy Nantucket.

He said to Zeke, "Maybe this was the last Atlantic whale? Maybe its jawbone was erected here by sailors as a memorial."

Zeke gave a small *wuff* in response.

"Maybe the single fisherman whose shack keeps a lookout over the arch found the bones and set it up by himself." Though given the size, he thought that highly unlikely.

Another *wuff* from Zeke.

"Maybe God set it there as a warning." Josiah did not know what kind of warning it might be. He knew he might never know. That silenced him.

The dog fell silent, too.

Suddenly, Josiah began shaking, for the wind had picked up. And the sun was quickly hidden behind a bank of clouds. Plus, his head was aching again, possibly from hunger, possibly from his labors, possibly still from the blow from the boom. Plus, it had been a long walk up and over the hill.

He thought briefly of turning back, but the thought of doing this walk twice was more than he could bear.

Perhaps there is some shelter in the shadow of that great arch. It was enough of a hope to get him moving again, in a kind of shambling, tumbling manner, till he fetched up against the left-hand part of the arch and sank down with his back resting against the bone.

He felt a kind of hum from the bone arch that seemed to go through his entire body, soothing the ache in his head. It could have been natural or magical. It did not matter. The hum made him feel better.

Josiah closed his eyes, fell asleep. And saw . . .

The Whale

In the beginning, the world was water. And then the Great Fluke dropped pieces in the water, pieces that humped out and stood in the way of a good, fast swim, pieces that sometimes one bumped a head on, or a fin or tail. But it was still mostly water.

And that was good.

Sometimes the cold ice came from the north and scoured the humps and lands, erratically dropping stones in our way. But we learned to swim around or swim farther, going toward the rise of the sun, till some of us lived on the far side of the big island and some on the near.

Though once a year, our young males would pilgrimage to the warmer waters to meet the family, and make new friends within the pods, and sometimes find mates.

And that was even more good.

For many years it was so, before the people came, small,

dark from the sun, who could not walk about without new skins, who could not cross water except in tree-boats, who had a hunger for meat creatures like us, and those creatures who ran on land or swam in the seas, or crawled into the tide pools or dug deep into tunnels, or sang through the air.

But it was still mostly good.

For we whales, leviathans as we were called at first, were large and hard to kill, and not all our meat was good in the new creatures' mouths.

Mostly they left us alone.

Until the day when they found we were good for more than just meat. For blubber and oil and bones. And then all the good went away, and we told stories and songs about those old and good days. And sang them to our children. And the deeps resounded with our songs. The rest is weeping and the sight of young whales swimming alone.

I am the door and the gateway. You have chosen to hear. There is more to this story if you listen. This island holds the key.

Josiah woke with a start. It had been a strange dream. About a door.

About a gateway.

About a key.

A key! He needed that key. It was the only way

into the fisherman's shack. He stood slowly, walking between each leg of the arch again and again, shuffling his feet and gazing at the ground. Eight times to either end, sixteen times in all.

Zeke was barking and then howling by the final time.

Josiah howled, too, shouting: "Foul Dream-gate. There *is* no key!"

Then he turned on his heel and headed back over the hill, past the shack, down the other side, till he came to the sandy patch where he had pulled up his boat. This time he pulled it even farther onto the seagrass, looking frantically for his sheathed knife and marlinspike, which were not there.

But stuffed back in the cuddy, where Zeke had originally kept them safe—he remembered that now—were his shoes and stockings.

"Good dog," he whispered hoarsely. Then he lay down with his dog under *Petrel*'s banged-up body. At least the boat kept off most of the wind.

"I promise thee," he told Zeke, "tomorrow we will eat *something*. We will think about where to go, what to do." He was too tired, too achy, to say more. His head had started to hurt again,

Zeke whimpered at the hoarseness of his boy's voice and snuggled closer.

As for Josiah, he wept for a while, but silently, so as not to disturb the dog further.

They were both hungry, scared, and exhausted, and as a result, slept like the dead, though still alive.

And without hope of a key.

Chapter Ten:
A Promise Worth Keeping

On the third day without food, their growling, aching stomachs woke them at the same time.

Crawling out from under the diminished catboat, Ezekiel and then Josiah stretched in the sun.

Sun, Josiah thought. *God's promise.* He looked down at Zeke and said, "This day we are breaking into that shack. It must be locked for some reason. Now!" He was surprised at how strong his voice was, considering . . .

Zeke looked surprised, too. Or perhaps he was surprised by the promise in his boy's voice.

Josiah walked down to the rocky shore and picked out three stones that fit like hammer heads in his hand. Then whistling for Zeke to follow, he went up the hill again to the desolate shack.

"Hope for a hammer, nails, fishing lines, and a new

sail," he said to Zeke, knowing he would be happy with even a few of those items. It was not as if he was going shopping with his mother in the Tucket General Store.

He'd not an ounce of guilt for what he was about to do, though *Thou Shalt Not Steal* still danced about in his empty stomach. He would replace any items when he was able to. He did not even think about getting home. It was one more day and one more day after that he had to consider. It was the way a dog thought. The way a fish or an ant—if they thought at all—thought. Or a whale.

And then Josiah remembered the whale in his odd dream. Possibly it was the whale whose jawbone stood guarding the gateway to home. A *fancy*, his mother would surely call it, like the fairy stories she used to read to him when he was a young boy. But that did not make it untrue.

He suddenly realized that Zeke was not at his heels, and when he turned to look back, the dog was nibbling on some grass stubble. Josiah dropped the three rocks and ran back, shouting: "No! No!"

But that was what Zeke always did when feeling ill. Eating grass gave him comfort. But short comfort, for he did what always came after—he briefly vomited up what bile still sat in his stomach.

By the time Josiah got to his dog's side, mere seconds, really, Zeke was done with the nibbling and into the rough part of this routine. His stomach heaved and then he gave a kind of cough. It was what Father called *hawking up*. First there was almost a cupful of whitish bile spurting from his mouth, followed by dribbles, and then a bit more. Drunk sailors did it. Father abhorred drunk sailors.

"Stupid dog," Josiah said, but tenderly, as he used the sleeve of his shirt to wipe the bile away. "Now come—we have work to do."

Zeke was not even a bit wobbly from his exertion, unlike the drunken sailors of Father's stories, but Josiah himself felt bit shaky. "I cannot do this alone, thee knows," he said to Zeke, meaning every word of it.

The dog looked at him as if he understood. There was a promise in his dark eyes.

They reached the place where Josiah had dropped the stones. One of them had shattered against a larger greyish rock that jutted from the earth, but the other two were sound.

Josiah let out a relieved breath. Zeke's head lowered as if in apology, and Josiah patted the dog's shoulder. "No worries, pup," he said, though the dog was almost as old as he. "That stone would have shattered on the door anyway. Best to find it out now."

And with those bold words to move them forward, they came again to the shack, which looked just as forlorn as the day before. Or even worse.

Suddenly Josiah felt as damaged and deserted as the shack. *Why would anyone leave* anything *on this forlorn island?* he thought. *Or build a shack on the top of a hill, where a hurricane could easily blow it off?*

And immediately he had a contrary idea: *Why lock up an empty shack?*

Suddenly, he understood that the shack's promise would remain a puzzle until he had it open. No need to worry about it till then. Not *Haste Makes Waste*, as Father had often quoted. It was the *now* that mattered, before he and the dog starved to death. Or died of the cold. Or . . .

It was important to get the blasted thing open. He lifted the first rock and slammed it against the lock.

It shattered. The rock, not the lock.

He looked at the rock in his other hand. It was exactly the same kind.

That would surely shatter, too. But he tried anyway.

Then he flung the bits of powdery rock away as far as he could, screaming at the same time, a string of curses that he had not known he knew. Not the words he had heard sailors say, but a strange combination of the plagues in the Old Testament and things he hated the most: thieving gulls, stinging insects, sharks that stole your catch, rocks that turned into dust when you needed them most.

Not surprisingly, it helped neither his situation nor his mood.

Wandering to the other side of the hill, he looked down where the bone arch stood defiantly upright in the soft wind.

He thought about home. About Nantucket. About houses with stone walls, and streets with stone cobbles, some crumbling, some solid. About walking through the woods with his father, who talked about granites as the hardest stones on the island, all the while pointing out greyish outcrops filled with what he called iron filings that shimmered and sometimes looked like brown rivers lazing through the gray stone.

Iron could help, Josiah thought. It was harder than stone.

But he also knew Nantucket, though thought of as a small island by the mainlanders, was huge compared to this one, where you could walk from one side or all around in an hour and a bit.

Well, he thought, *in an hour when I am not vomiting bile or having a clanging headache or a stomach that contracts with each hunger pain.*

And then he thought: *Would there be granites here?* But he had no one on this No Man's Island to ask.

And then, oddly, he remembered that only the week

before, at First Day's Meeting, his mother had risen to speak.

I tell thee the truth; Matthew 17:20, she'd said, *as does Matthew, that if thee has faith even as small as the size of a mustard seed, thee will say to this mountain, 'Move from here to there,' and it will move; nothing will be impossible for thee.*

She had been speaking of a problem on Nantucket. But wouldn't it be true on this small island as well?

Since he had no one to ask, he would have to walk the whole thing and see for himself. He had at least that much faith—the size of a mustard seed. Maybe even the size of a canning jar of mustard.

Whistling to Zeke, who came reluctantly to his side, Josiah said, "We stick together, thee and me. And that's a promise."

The dog's answer was a slow wag of his tail as if he were too sick or too tired to wag harder.

And that, Josiah told himself, *is a kind of promise as well.*

CHAPTER ELEVEN:
Shack Attack

Most of the stones on the way to the shack were the same layered material as the stones he'd tried before. But the more inland he went, the more there seemed to be a smattering of the gray stone his father had pointed out to him, a year or so before. Unfortunately, they were all were part of larger stones buried deep in the ground. Without digging tools, he had no way to unearth them.

He tried not to be discouraged, and with his dog trotting at his side, their stomachs growling in a kind of companiable syncopation, he found he could almost, though not quite, enjoy the walk. For the sun was out, the breeze barely a wisp.

"A good day to die," he whispered to Zeke, "but a better day to live."

And just as he announced that, he saw ahead of them a scattering of gray stones, not quite as far as the Arch, but close, catching the light.

Almost as if someone had thrown them there to be found.

He stopped for a moment to catch his breath, to give both of them time to breathe in hope. Also, time for him to listen to the still, small voice that he had never truly heard before.

And there, all unexpected, was a voice in his ear, saying, "You asked for stones instead of food. I give you both."

It might have just been a wish, a desire, a reason to move forward with hope, and not despair. But he heard it as a distinct voice. Not Mother's or Father's familiar voices. Not the harbormaster's deep, advising baritone. Nor his friends' lighter chatter. This was some voice unknown to him, an overwhelming presence of a voice.

He thought of running away from it, but he was all out of breath. So was Zeke.

Instead, they walked quickly, quietly over to the stones that shimmered on the path, stones that Josiah had not noticed the day before, because he had not thought he needed them. Or didn't remember such stones existed, or because it had been an overcast day and no sun made them shine. Or . . . perhaps they simply had not been there at the time. That thought made him shiver with a kind of wordless fear.

Most of the stones were humps of buried boulders, but three were hand-sized chunks, lying far apart from one another, like distant cousins who no longer spoke.

Josiah knelt down as if praying, and perhaps he was. Though Quakers did not kneel for prayer, but stood tall when they witnessed at Meeting.

He reached for one of the stones, and it was solid in his hand. He went over to the next. By the third, he had no more hands to hold them, so he shrugged out of his shirt and put them in it like a sack. Then he swung the sack onto his back, turned, and started up the hill.

Zeke took a moment to understand what Josiah was doing, before racing after him, joy in his every bounding step. By the time they reached the hilltop, they were both galloping and soon out of breath again.

Josiah stopped and sat down, and Zeke immediately flopped by his side, panting. Opening his improvised sack, Josiah looked at the three rocks again. They had not lost any particles and seemed impenetrable. But he knew they must have once been part of the larger boulders. He could not quite let go of doubt. Or fear, which had only just entered his vocabulary and still had its icy hand on his bare shoulder.

And then he said, without thinking more, "Let's do

this!" and stood. Zeke got up, too, and they walked slowly over to the front of the shack.

Methodically, Josiah set the three stones down by the door. Then he shook out his shirt to rid it of any shards of stone, even though he could see none.

Picking up the smallest of the rocks, the one that fit perfectly in his hand, he took a deep breath and slammed it against the lock, expecting nothing.

The lock made a loud sound, almost a death knell. Then it fell off the door handle onto the ground, landing near the larger two stones.

Zeke went over and sniffed it, as if it were some sort of dead animal, possibly edible. But Josiah promptly dropped to the ground in front of the shack with an audible grunt, as if all of his doubts—which had been the only things actually propping him up—had suddenly left him.

The voice had promised stones and had given them. Surely food would not be far behind.

"Thank thee," Josiah whispered, almost crying. "Thank thee."

But then his old passenger, doubt, reminded him from afar: *stones are easy, but food kept in an old shack might not be edible. In fact, it might possibly kill you both.*

Josiah didn't dare hope, and yet he did. Standing up again, with great effort, he slowly opened the shack door and stared at what lay before him.

Not a grand larder. Not tools, weapons, nor various foods. But two fishing nets, some ropes, a small bailing pail, and an old, beaten-up fisherman's raincoat.

When he tried the coat on, it was for someone possibly twice his size. But that mattered little. Yes, it was heavy and long. But that was good. He and Zeke would sleep well and warm that night.

But right now, he thought, *what we really need . . .*

"We're going fishing, Zeke," Josiah said. And even if they had to eat the fish uncooked and cold, at least they would not starve.

As if he understood, Zeke gave a sharp yip and came over to be petted.

Filled with hope and a small amount of joy, the two of them trotted back down the hill and over to where *Petrel* lay, dry-moored in the grass. They left the coat and pail by the boat, but took the rope and both nets down to the rocky shore that had marooned them.

It was low tide. They could walk out onto the flats.

Josiah was not a dab hand at fishing with a net. Mostly he and his friends used lines and hooks and fished from wharves. But he certainly had seen it done, though always from a boat where the fisherman dropped the nets over into deep water.

But as he had no boat fit to sail, he would have to walk into the tide. He knotted the lightest of the ropes onto two sides of the smaller net, and then the larger net, both with knots his father had taught him. Then he took off his shoes and stockings and his trousers, and off he and Zeke went, the dog in the lead.

The water was cold, but Josiah was on fire with the thoughts of catching something for them to eat. And when he was ankle-high in the water, with Zeke several paces behind, he swung the nets over his head and let them fly out to sea, though holding tight to the end of the rope.

As the nets sank down into the tide, only the rope, now attached at the other end to Josiah's wrist, showed where they had gone. Boy and dog watched carefully. Not just this day's dinner depended upon those nets. Survival did as well.

Zeke began barking eagerly, but the nets were too far out in the water for him to venture after them. He waded in till his knees were just barely covered, growling a bit, as if the nets were live things.

Josiah left the nets drift down for a moment, then began hauling them back to the shore. They did not feel particularly heavy, and he guessed there were no fish this time. But still he had to look.

He was right. There was nothing in either of the nets.

The next two throws returned only flotsam: bits of weeds and a small stick, stuff too tiny to be either useful or edible.

Zeke growled at the empty nets and began to walk stiff-legged back to the overturned boat, presumably to take a nap in its shade. But hearing the sound of the wet nets being flung out again, he turned to watch, this time from afar.

The fourth time, Josiah went a bit farther out, as far as his waist. Suddenly his left foot could not find anywhere to stand. A drop-off of land!

He backed up quickly, knowing he was lucky not to have gone under.

Once sure-footed again, he cried out: "For thee, Zeke!" Then he flung the nets wide into the tide. This time the nets went out over the deeper water.

Please . . . please . . . Josiah thought. Less a plea than a prayer.

Almost immediately he felt something exploring the strands of the nets.

From inside, he hoped, *not just outside.* Pulling quickly on the rope, he felt it close up the gaping top.

When he got back to the shore, there were three rather dismal scup caught in the net. He brought them up to the grass and spread the big coat over them to keep away the noisy, always hungry gulls.

"We eat today," he told Zeke, and *this* the dog

seemed to understand, because he nosed at the coat eagerly.

Not willing to leave the starving dog alone with a possible feast, Josiah decided not to chance going out into the water again. Especially because he was feeling the cold. So, he climbed under the coat with Zeke, smashed each fish on the head with one of the granite rocks, and then with trembling fingers ripped the scup apart. Careless of any bones, he divided the meat equally between the dog and himself.

Zeke finished his share first, in three quick gulps, so of course, Josiah redivided the small bits he had left with his dog. Then he sat a while in thought and digestion, hoping his shrunken stomach would not repel the bits of uncooked fish.

On the way back out of the water with the netted scup, he'd spotted a small estuary running up the side of the island. On Nantucket, such an estuary almost always housed groups of shellfish: clams, oysters, littlenecks. And though it was early in the season for them to be at their largest and sweetest, he hoped he might be lucky enough to find a few around. Though enough to make a full meal? Doubtful.

Besides, he had no fire to cook them. No tongs for prying them off the rocks. It might be really hard work gathering enough for a meal. And trying to open clams with a granite rock might ruin the meat inside. But he knew he had to try because he and the dog were still hungry. Zeke was licking all sides of the net now.

There was still plenty of daylight enough to try the estuary. Besides, his mother always said: "Nothing ventured, nothing gained."

So, venture it would be!

He got back into his shirt and pants, all the while considering the odds of finding such a trove.

Perhaps, Josiah thought, *this estuary also has fresh water coming in farther along*. He knew that he and the dog would not get far by counting on rain to fill the large bailer from the boat, and the small bucket they'd found, with fresh water. And he suddenly recalled his father saying that lack of fresh water would kill a man faster than starvation.

A man, Josiah thought. *What about a boy or a dog?*

Picking up two of the granite stones, he went back to the rocks, easily found the estuary, and began walking slowly, trousers rolled way up, knee-deep in the water.

He put away expectations and hope, concentrating on not tripping, falling, or breaking a toe.

It took over a hundred paces until he found what he could only have dreamed about the night before—a tiny group of littlenecks in the estuary bottom. *Quahogs*, the natives had called them, or so said his father. Funny he should remember that now. Finding them was lucky, too, for unlike oysters, they did not cling desperately to rocks, but could be picked up out of the mud.

Josiah and his friends often treaded out littlenecks with their bare feet when on familiar ground, but here, by himself, on an unnamed island and in an estuary he was just getting to know, he had to be careful testing the water bottoms with bare feet.

Though what that could be worse than being marooned far from home with a broken boat and not even knowing how far away home was.

Starving, a little voice told him. *Starving is worse.* He refocused on the food.

The quahogs were quite small, but he knew if he didn't eat them, the gulls surely would. He actually preferred clams and regular oysters, which made more of a meal, but with neither knife nor marlinspike to get those off the rocks they clung to, clams and oysters would be a lot more work than they were worth.

Luckily, he found half a dozen of the littlenecks and carried them back to the overturned boat, where he knocked them about with the rock and pulled out the small bits of meat inside. He didn't feel the scratches on his two longest fingers but he did see them, though that was long after his meal.

Even with all that hard work, the meal was well worth it. Littlenecks eaten fresh out of the water had a salty taste. His mother on special occasions melted a bit of butter to put on top. But mostly they went directly into the chowder pot.

Of course, he and Zeke had to eat them raw, cows not being an option on the little island. Or a butter churn. Or, alas—and more important—fire.

And if raw shellfish looks a bit like snot, he thought, which Rayburn had once said on an estuary outing, *I can just close my eyes.*

The littlenecks certainly didn't taste like his mother's chowder. If they tasted like anything, it was lobster not boiled long enough in the cookpot. But it was food, as the voice had promised—stones and food. Though the voice hadn't made it clear that both were to come together! Josiah spat out a small bit of sand or maybe stone.

Thinking of his mother's chowder, though, made him think once again about her. He wondered if she had begun to worry yet, or just thought he was sulking at a friend's overnight. Perhaps she was too caught up in Ishmael Black's tale to wonder why Josiah had not returned. Or weeping too hard for the loss of her husband to worry about the loss of her son.

He pushed all thoughts of his mother aside and just hoped he and Zeke could keep the food down long enough to ease their hunger. And this hope, at least, proved providential.

They slept long and well and warm all that night. Except . . . except for something that poked at Josiah in the middle of his sleep. Something that made him turn over, but not enough to wake him from his dreams of home to do anything about it. And when he woke in the morning, he had forgotten the poking had happened at all.

Or the dreams.

CHAPTER TWELVE:
Late Spring's Promise

The days moved slowly, but the weeks turned over fast. Josiah was not sure how that happened. But he established a rhythm to his days, finding fresh water at the estuary three times a day, and fishing (scup and the occasional cunner, with its super sharp teeth and musky taste which Zeke loved, but Josiah ate while holding his nose and complaining). They also gobbled up littleneck clams when they could. It was a boring once-a-day meal, but they had both gotten used to it.

Josiah decided he needed to give himself regular chores, so he made a list in his head. On what he considered Second Days (only because he called it that, not because he knew which day was which), he tried liberating larger clams and oysters from the rocks. Mostly without success.

On Third Days he walked the entire island, picking

up anything he thought might be useful—small tree limbs that had floated onto their shores in case he might ever be able to start a fire, plus a few more granite rocks until he had enough for a firepit.

Once he even found a dead duck washed up on one of the outer rocks and waded in after it at an exceptionally low tide. Using one of the smaller pieces of wood and a granite stone, he managed to peel back the skin. But when he ate a bit of raw meat off the breastbone, he threw up so quickly that he left the rest for Zeke and the gulls, who made short work of it.

"Better stomachs than mine," he told himself ruefully.

On Fourth Days, he visited the Arch where he sat, trying to think his way through the puzzle of his new life. On the one hand, he and his dog were still healthy enough. Both quite thin, of course, but eating fish, occasional clams, and drinking enough fresh water kept them fed and moving about.

Fifth Days he mostly dedicated to playing with the dog. They were both quite adept at fetching sticks by now. It didn't matter what he threw: twigs, tree limbs, or an unopened shellfish. As long as he called out "Fetch!" the game always continued. And Zeke never tired of it first.

Sixth Days were set aside to consider his three most difficult problems: food, fire, and escape. If he thought about them more often than that, he grew morose and sometimes even broke into tears. But by dedicating a single day to the problem, he was quite able to stay hopeful. Especially about being rescued.

On Seventh Days, he thought about his mother as well. Since it had been over a month, and heading into summer, with no boats even passing by or trying to land on his desolate island, he had to assume she had forgotten all about him. She must have thought him dead, for surely if she thought him living, she would have gathered a fleet of boats from his friends and the Meeting to search for him.

Or possibly she didn't care at all, and was already remarried. Perhaps to Ishmael Black, and uninterested in even finding her son's body. That thought rankled so much, Josiah rarely let himself consider it.

Or, perhaps she married one of the rich old widowers on the island, though none came immediately to mind.

He wished her well sometimes, and was angry at other times. Seventh Day was always an uncomfortable day.

The thing that worried him the most was not how he was doing *now*.

Now he was able to treat the island as a hideaway, a spring and summer retreat. The chores he chose to do were his own, as if he owned the island and not because it kept him a prisoner. But what would happen once autumn set in—*that* was worrying. And winter. He had pushed winter far away from his mind.

In reality, he knew he had been so focused on finding food and staying warm he had often forgotten—or pointedly did not let himself think about—leaving the island on his own. It required too many steps, and if only one went wrong, he and Zeke could be in more danger than now.

Rescue was a simpler, cleaner, less dangerous way to get off the isle. Perhaps he needed to consider ways of making their presence known and noticeable to any passing ships.

Only occasionally on Seventh Days, he thought: *Leave the island for what?* He had no answer for that. Except . . . except there was no way he and Zeke could live here during a New England winter. And even if there was, even if he could figure out how to make and keep a fire going—why would he want to? If he got off the island, he could possibly apprentice himself to someone on the mainland, he could work on a lobster boat, he could . . . but here he was beholden to no one. It was a puzzle he could not solve, a knot he could not untie.

But once again, each Seventh Day, when the sun shone bright overhead, he pushed all those thoughts aside, certain that he would be rescued soon.

As for First Days, because the practice was so en-
grained in his Nantucket life, he went to a Quaker
Meeting of two. He sat on a log that he had dragged
for his unused firepit but was, for now, a bench in his
own meetinghouse under the sky. He would sit for
nearly an hour every island First Day, except when it
rained, Zeke quietly at his feet, waiting for that silent
voice to come to him again and tell him what to do
next. Though the only voice he heard, other than his
own, was the dog's.

Neither of them had much to say that was helpful.

But this being a Fifth Day, and a beautiful summer
day at that, Josiah and Zeke walked over the hill to the
Arch and sat down beneath it.

Josiah liked to look up to the very spot where the
front of the whale's mouth would have been, and
think about it gaping open, then closing. He still could
not figure out whether it was the bottom part of the
whale's jaw or the top. Or how many men it must
have taken to set it there or why. But when the sky
was this blue and cloudless, it did not seem to matter.

"I suppose," he said to Zeke, who attended to
his every word, "the only place it would be useful
knowing the top from the bottom would be in the

sea." He considered that for a moment, and added, "By the time we were close enough to figure it out, it would be too late. We would be a pair of Jonahs without an escape plan." He laughed at his own joke. The noise he made sounded creaky. He hadn't laughed in quite a while. And then, thinking about his father and that white whale, he realized the joke was not funny at all and had to work hard not to weep.

The dog seemed to agree, shoving his nose into Josiah's neck, which led to them wrestling a bit as they'd often done before. Before Ishmael Black. Before Josiah had run off. Before the boom hit his head. Before *Petrel* crashed. Before . . .

Then Josiah scooted over to one of the legs of the arch, set his back to it, closed his eyes, and took a nap. For the second time, he fell into a wild dream. Not about a talking whale this time, or the island, or his mother, or Nantucket. He dreamed about a whaling ship.

Dream Two:
The Doubloon

The first mate stands on the deck, staring at something on the mast. From the side, his face looks fathoms long. But still Josiah cannot see what it is that makes his father look so grim. Then his father turns, shoulders pulled back, as if to give himself strength, as if he has made a hard decision.

And now—now! Josiah can see what has made him so angry. It is something round and gold tacked to a mast. Much too large and shiny for a Nantucket coin. Could it possibly be a gold doubloon? Josiah has only heard of such wealth, a coin made in South America, a piece so valuable it lived in palaces and cathedrals, but not on a ship's mast where anyone might steal it.

"Because what is hammered in," his father muses aloud, "can be spiked out again."

Josiah looks closer, as if the dream is a telescope and his is the only eye. Now he can read what is on the face of the large coin. But it makes no more sense to him than an enchanter's incantation—REPÚBLICA DEL ECUADOR: QUITO.

He lets the words roll around in his mouth, but no magic happens.

Except now his father's recognizable hand—large and eloquent, with its black stone ring—appears over the coin, fingers spread as if to efface the gold. For the life of him, Josiah cannot guess why.

But then he hears a shout from someone he does not know. Though whose voice but his father's would he know, anyway, even in a dream?

"Ship ahoy! Hast thee seen the bloody white whale?" the voice calls. And the view shifts in the dream so that Josiah can see a ship showing English colors bearing down on them. The captain so addressing them is a darkly tanned and burly man, sixty years or so, with a jacket that sports one empty sleeve streaming behind him like a kite's tail caught in the wind.

Josiah thinks it is all as mysterious and as watchable as a group of actors on a touring stage, and he the sole audience, though he has but once seen such a spectacle on Nantucket and failed to tell his parents about it.

"See you this!" cries the unknown captain, holding up a white arm made of sperm whale bone, very like the bone under Josiah's head as he sleeps, only much, much smaller, of course, as if the maker had used a whale's rib, not an entire jaw. The bone ends in a wooden head, like a mallet.

One could drive a nail through a doubloon with that, Josiah thinks, if one had a doubloon. And a mast.

"*Compliments of that very whale,*" *the English captain says. He speaks crisply, not at all like a New Englander.*

"*An old Englander,*" *Josiah says, laughing to himself.*

"*Then come aboard; we have tales to swap,*" *says the nearer captain, now stomping into view. He has a single true leg and one carved of bone.*

Josiah knows this nearer captain. Ahab, of the Pequod.

The sailors on the Pequod *haul the burly man aboard so the two captains—one with a missing arm, the other with a missing leg—can have a parley. About white whales.*

"*Spin me a yarn about thy arm,*" *Captain Ahab says, giving a smile that has little warmth in it.* "*And tell me if ye have seen that white monstrosity again.*"

Two sailors hop to, bringing two stools, and the two captains sit, leaning forward, head-to-head.

"*And have ye seen it again?*" *Ahab repeats.* "*The white whale?*"

"*Twice,*" *the other man says, but does not further elaborate.*

"*But ye could not fasten either time?*" *Ahab asks, with clear disdain in his voice.*

"*Ain't one limb enough?*" *the other man asks.*

Ahab does not look amused, mumbling, "*He is a magnet for all that.*" *Then he stands and stomps off. It is a brutal dismissal. A snub. Even Josiah understands that.*

The English captain turns to one of the sailors, a dark-skinned

*fellow, maybe Ishmael Black's cannibal, who bends low to listen.
"Is your captain crazy?"*

*If the sailor answers, Josiah does not hear because neither of
them interest him further, and the dream shifts so that he can
find his father, who has been watching all this from the deck.
His father turns and, several steps behind, follows the seething
Ahab. Josiah has to trot to keep up with them, but he remains
unseen and unheard by all.*

*They go into the captain's cabin, where Ahab turns on his
first mate. "And ye, Starbuck, said nothing there in my de-
fense?"*

*His father's name in Ahab's mouth sounds dirty, shameful,
like a curse.*

*The captain rolled on. "Yet ye prate to me all the time, Star-
buck, about those miserly owners, as if they are my conscience.
Well, they are not and ye are not. Ye Quakers, so high and holy.
But know this—the only real owner of any ship is its commander.
And hark ye, my only conscience is in this ship's keel."*

*Josiah waits for his father to refute this, to say that Ahab's
insistence on killing the white whale feels like a death march for
the men in his care. Not just Ahab's own death. And by what
right does he have to command that?*

*The captain's voice is punishingly loud. His words are clearly
meant to demean, embarrass, hurt. However, all his father says
to this is, "A better man than I might pass over in thee what he
would resent in a younger man . . ."*

But before his father can get into a deeper reproach, if that is his intention, the captain moves up close, cutting him off: "Dost thou dare to criticize me? Who is captain here? Who is mate?" *Ahab spits out the words, and they splatter in his first mate's face, on his collar, as if the ocean itself is castigating Starbuck.*

Josiah watches in horror as his father shrinks into silence, something his mother would never have done. Speak Truth to Power. *That is the watchword of all Quakers.*

His father's silence makes no sense to Josiah. "Father!" *he breathes out in warning.*

As if his unheard voice stiffens his father's resolve for one more try, Josiah hears him say to the captain, "Nay, sir—I do not criticize, I entreat. Shall we not understand each other better than hitherto, Captain?"

Ahab does not immediately speak, but seizes a loaded pistol from a rack and points it at Starbuck. "There is one God that is Lord over the earth, and one captain that is lord over the Pequod. *Get ye back on deck.*"

"Father . . ." *Josiah warns again, for his father's cheeks have turned a fiery red, and he takes a step towards the captain, his right hand beginning to fist. But then, as if mastering his emotion, he swivels and leaves the cabin instead.*

Josiah lets out the breath he hadn't realized he was holding, but dutifully trails after his father, who has stopped for a moment in the doorway.

Josiah stops, too.

But then his father, like an actor on the stage, looks back, looks through Josiah, but does not see him. He remarks only to the captain, "Let Ahab beware of Ahab." And then he leaves.

Josiah waits for a second or two to listen further. There is something more from the captain, whose remarks trail after his first mate, who is already down the hall.

"He waxes brave," the captain says sneeringly, "but nevertheless obeys, a most careful bravery, that . . ."

And to his misery and shame, Josiah agrees.

And then he woke and looked about. The sky was darkening. Surely it was too early for night to be drawing in. He felt a shudder in the wind.

Ah, he thought. *There's going to be another blow.* He whistled to Zeke, who had been faithfully dozing by his feet.

"Back to the catboat," Josiah said, standing, a bit wobbly, as if having to find his land legs again. And not just from the rocking of the *Pequod*, but from the knocking of his own traitor heart.

They would have to shelter under *Petrel*, surrounded by all the things they'd collected, and wait out the rain. It looked to be a major storm, the first one since the storm that had driven them onto the rocks and left them on this hidden isle.

CHAPTER THIRTEEN:
The Next Big Blow

Josiah and Zeke turned as one to look behind, where the darkening sky was racing toward them, almost too fast to be real. He wondered if he was still in the dream, but even if so, it did not matter. Inside the dream or out, the two of them needed to shelter from the storm. It threatened to be a big blow.

Climbing back up the hill, Josiah thought about waiting it out in the shack. The black sky was almost upon them. It was that quick.

Ezekiel had already galloped on ahead, and Josiah knew he had to be with the dog. They were partners in this adventure, and did not dare become separated.

So, after stopping for just a second to catch his next breath, and knowing downhill would be the easier run, Josiah began racing after Zeke.

By the time he got to the bottom of the hill, the rain had already started pattering down, but the wind had not hit them yet. So, Josiah took a moment to gather the sticks he had been saving for tinder and possible work on the boat and brought them under *Petrel*'s sheltering planks. Then he wiggled into the oversized coat and lay down, his arms around his shivering dog. And just in time.

Zeke was already trembling uncontrollably with fear, so, keeping his voice soothing and steady, Josiah muttered nursery rhymes into his dog's ears until the worst of the winds had subsided.

He had no idea how long he spoke. Minutes? Hours? Half a day? He only knew the coat kept the worst of the rain off their backs and the overturned boat kept them out of the wind.

Well, mostly.

He thought the noise the wind made sounded like sailors screaming when a whale stove in the side of their boat. Or perhaps it was what sinners sounded like in the bowels of Hell.

He kept reminding himself that he and Zeke were safer under the overturned boat on the shore than out in the boat on the water. But the more Josiah thought about it, the more he realized how vulnerable they were, their only shelter a small boat missing two boards on an island without trees. Vulnerable to wind and rain and lightning strikes. If the sea rose, even more vulnerable, for the only high spot on the island was a hill with a shack using most of the space there.

Soon, he had talked himself into shivering as much as the dog.

When the storm finally passed over, the quiet was in some ways even more frightening, for the gulls and other water birds were also silent.

It is the silence, he thought, *of a battlefield with the dead, the only ones still left unshriven, unburied, unmourned.* For the first time, he really wondered if he would ever see Nantucket again. Or his mother. Or his friends. And on that scary note, he fell asleep at last, the dog firmly in his arms.

The storm hammering on the bottom of the upturned boat did not wake them, nor the moan of the sea as it climbed ever closer to their makeshift bedroom. The sky held its lightning rods close and decided not to fling those loud harpoons down at them.

For a big blow, it was over remarkably fast. But they did not know that. Fear and exhaustion had kept them in the thrall of sleep.

When they woke to a gray dawn, the dog was moaning as if hurt, not just afraid. That was when Josiah discovered that there was something wrong indeed, and that *something* was poking into Zeke's side, as it had poked in Josiah's side days before. Something in the coat.

He lifted the side of the boat and rolled out onto the soggy grass, the coat in hand, trying hard not to wake the dog, who had ceased moaning.

Once standing, Josiah put a hand in each of the deep pockets of the fisherman's coat, though he found nothing in either one. However, there was a substantial hole in the left pocket.

He felt around the lining of the coat in case something had slipped through the hole. There was definitely something hard there, near the bottom. *Maybe*, he prayed, *a knife? A marlinspike?* He took off the coat and, careful not to make the hole any bigger, felt down—way down.

His fingers touched something cold, like steel. But not sharp like a knife, nor rounded like a marlinspike. It took nearly a minute more, dropping it twice, before he could pull the odd thing out.

It looked like nothing more than a steel tooth from a garden rake. His mother had one for her vegetable patch. No wonder it was uncomfortable to sleep on. No wonder Zeke had complained. But Josiah knew at once what it was.

A fire striker!

Father had one for his boat. Along with the newfangled lucifers, of course. But he had always sworn by the fire striker, saying often: "Lucifers can get wet and then will no longer work, or they can run out, but an iron fire striker will never fail."

Last time he had said that, it had been a day when they were off on a jaunt together, which was right before he left on the *Pequod*.

Fire striker! A piece of iron you could strike against flint, chert, marble, or other stones. It might take a while to find out which stones were here on the island. Besides, he was not that certain which stones were which. Still, he could work with the striker until they had a fire going. If he had nothing else, Josiah knew he had time!

They would be having a hot meal this night. Of *that* he was certain.

He put the fire striker back under the boat, as if hiding it from any intruder who might want to steal it. As if an intruder could ever be found.

"Come on, Zeke," he said to the dog, who nuzzled his way to another patch of wet grass to do his morning business. "We have some more exploring to do."

Wagging his long, lean tail, the dog eagerly followed as Josiah went down to the shore where they had first been thrown onto the island.

The tide was still pretty high, but on its way out, and there was a lot of flotsam from the storm. Josiah wasn't too particular. Anything that looked interesting he grabbed from the waves. Anything he considered useless could always be thrown back.

Stuck in the rocks was half of a battered bailing pail, but still possibly useful, and an entire tree branch also within reach. He leaned over for it, almost losing his balance, but managed to catch himself in time.

"Careful," he whispered. "One bad fall and . . ."

The caution didn't stop him from trying again, this time with the help of Zeke, who leaped in and grabbed a part of the tree limb with his mouth, soaking them both in the process, but they got the entire tree branch to the shore.

"When we find the right rock to start a fire," Josiah told him, "the first bite of cooked littlenecks goes to thee!"

Zeke's tail wagged hard, as if he understood. And perhaps he did. Certainly, Josiah's mood was infectious.

The rest of what they pulled in was useless, except for the tree limb and the half pail, both of which he stored far up on the shore.

Clearly Zeke thought that they were playing a game

of fetch, for he went back in after each bit of flotsam Jake threw in. On the sixth romp, he went head over heels into a deep hole, popping up again and looking more drowned than alive. Josiah waded in and pulled the coughing, shivering dog out.

As he moved carefully back to shore, his bare foot struck something sharp. "Ow!" he cried aloud, dropping the dog into the water, which was only ankle deep there.

Josiah's face twisted with pain as Zeke, yipping, raced onto the shore, barking his complaints.

Josiah was certain he'd sliced his big toe on a sharp rock, a stupid, careless thing to have done. He had had no bandages at hand, nor his mother's homemade ointments. No doctors to call on him. Trying to find out what had sliced his toe, Josiah carefully reached down.

When he stood up again, gazing at the object in his hand, his mouth was wide open, and his mouth opened wide in amazement and delight. It was the remains of his sheath, now badly torn from being tugged out from beneath a rock, but still managing to cling to both knife and marlinspike. It had been the knife poking out the bottom of the useless sheath that had cut his toe. And—as he realized once they were ashore and examined his foot more closely—not even badly cut. More like a poke than a slice.

Josiah limped back to the upturned boat with the

sheath held tightly in his left hand as if at any moment, it might turn and run back into the sea, while Zeke, sniffing for a moment but not sure what it meant, followed closely at his heels.

Josiah knelt by the boat and pulled out the fire striker from its hiding place. Then he lined up striker, sheath, knife, and marlinspike in a row on the ground.

"These," he said solemnly to Zeke, who had come over to sniff the catch. The dog looked unimpressed.

"These will save our lives. Or at least give us a chance to get home."

At the word "home," the dog's tailed ticked back and forth like a school metronome during music lessons.

"*If* we want to go home," Josiah added. "*If* there is anyone at home who wants us there." Even to his own ears that seemed ill said, and unfounded. But as if to convince himself, he said it again. "Even if no one wants us there."

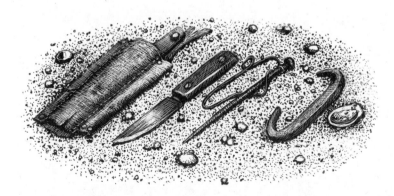

Zeke's tail kept wagging until Josiah had to give in to its good mood. "Come on ,then," he said. "Let's *really* go clamming!"

He grabbed the larger bailing bucket as well as the just-found, battered half pail. He loaded in the striker, marlinspike, and knife. As an afterthought, he added the sheath to use as a kind of leather finger guard, should he need it.

Then off they went with the certainty of success for the first time since being wrecked on the island. Or at least, Josiah felt that way, and his good mood translated into a bounding dog by his side.

Chapter Fourteen:
Idyll

The estuary lay like a long pantry before them. And with the spike and knife, it was simple to pry the clams from the rocks, along with their old and only favorite, the littlenecks. Josiah was giddy with the idea of all the different tastes.

"Once we get these back to the camp," he said to Zeke, "the tide will be heading out, and it will be safe enough to go fishing with our nets."

He also realized how much more food they would have that night, and not just because they were able to carry more food back with the two pails. But also because they would be able to get the clams without destroying a good deal of the meat by having to smash the shells.

"And cooked, too!" he cried out to Zeke, who barked back. "A feast!"

"O knife," he whispered. "O spike!" As if that were a prayer.

He looked down at the two pails jammed with what they had found, thinking: *Enough for lunch* and *dinner.* Before today, two meals in one day had been unthinkable.

They followed the estuary back to camp, where Josiah set aside a bunch of the smaller limbs from the recently rescued tree branch, breaking what he could with his bare hands and sawing off the slightly larger pieces with his knife, though he preferred to save the knife for more important work.

He put half of those limbs and the now-dry leafy bits in the firepit.

Bits of bark, scattered leaves, and the tips of some cattails that he'd found growing by the estuary—all would make what his father called a "bird's nest," though not an actual one. It would cradle the start of his fire. When he had a big enough nest, with an actual hollow, he left it in the pit.

Then they went back up the estuary to where the water was clearer, fresher, and less salty. There, he filled the big bailed to the top.

———

Once back by the boat and firepit, Josiah opened half of the clams, which, with knife and marlinspike, was easy to do.

"Thank thee, Father," he whispered, "for the knife and marlinspike, and teaching me the use of them." He hoped that a shimmer in the air or a throat clearing would let him know his father was near, but expected nothing.

Nothing was what he got. But he was satisfied, nonetheless.

Then he knelt on one knee with the fire striker in his left hand, the marlinspike in his right, remembering what his father had showed him about starting fires, and how to use the striker against either knife or marlinspike. The quick, sharp scrape that spat out sparks. In this case, it worked best on the rougher surface of the marlinspike.

And then his father had shown him how the sparks had to be directed into the nest of leaves and bark, which—as parts were still a bit wet—took longer than he had hoped to flame.

But flame it finally did. He put it quickly under the pile of sticks.

When the first of the wood began to smoke, he had blown into it with short, steady puffs. Then the branches caught fire, and eventually the water in the bailer started to bubble and boil. Soon, the clams began to open, and he danced around and around the pit like a madman, followed by his barking dog.

Finally, tiring, he stirred the clams in the bailer, lifting the shells out with the knife, and then leaned over to sniff the mist from the bailer. The smell brought him pure joy.

He stirred the cooking clams with the knife. Of course, he couldn't make clam chowder. Not like his mother's. Without bacon or butter or onion, or potatoes, or flour or cream or . . . he was remembering his mother's chowder simmering. The best in Nantucket, his father always said. As good the second day as the first.

But these clams and littlenecks, stewed in salt and fresh water after days of picking out crumbles of rock and eating them raw, was the next best thing to her delicious chowder. Cooked clams, even without being chowder, along with the seasoning of his doubts, made the meal even sweeter.

Oh, Mother, he thought. *Perhaps I have misjudged thee. Perhaps.*

And now that he had fire—anything was possible.

He and Zeke stuffed themselves till they could hardly move. But there was still food left over, which they could reheat or have cold for their evening meal.

Josiah put the half-full bailer inside the boat and pulled the boat down over to keep it safe for later.

Then they walked around the island, for pleasure this time, not for food. And when they got to the Arch, both he and Zeke fell asleep with their backs against an arch leg.

It took only a little while before Josiah began to dream. An unsettling dream that upon waking, felt absolutely true, yet he could not believe it. In fact, he refused to believe it. He was not sure why.

DREAM THREE:
Nantucket Sleigh Ride

*I*n the dream, he sees the whaling ship, but she is too far away
for him to swim to, nor can he read her name from where he
is. So, he does not know if it is the Pequod or not, though it
has a familiar look to it.

He is sitting in a large oared boat with other men, a harpooner standing up at the prow. He knows that is what the man
is because of the weapon in his hand, an odd spear with double
flukes. Josiah thinks the shaft is perhaps five or six feet long.
However, that's naught but a pin's length compared to Leviathan. Surely the men do not mean to defeat the whale with such
a small stick.

The harpooner in his boat is a wiry, medium-sized man.
Josiah wonders if he might be an Indian because his skin is the
same color as Abram Quary's.

He glances quickly to both port and starboard. The men in
the boat look around as well, but in a different direction, for

they sit backwards so the boat can propel forward, the harpooner at the front.

The boat is one of three small boats, a convoy or a covey of them, each with a harpooner in the prow.

Josiah glances quickly at the other two harpooners standing in the prows of the other boats. They are strangers to him, of course, both nearly naked. Their harpoons are of a similar length.

He thinks: Thee could kill a man with such a spear! Thee could bring down a wolf, or even a black bear, with one, perhaps. But a whale? *Dream Josiah is not convinced. Even three of those sticks do not make the length or breadth of a whale. None are big enough to kill one outright. Perhaps just anger him.*

These smaller whaleboats are not powered by sails when they are on the close hunt, but by oars, which the men ply with rippling swiftness, as if they are the wind over choppy water.

Strangely, although he himself is not rowing, no one seems to notice Josiah or comment upon him. It is how he knows for certain that this is a dream.

Suddenly an oarsman at the prow of the boat cries out, "Thar! Thar she blows! And thar again! The gold doubloon is mine! Mine!" And at his cry all the men in all the small boats row faster than before.

"Pull, ye hearties, for Captain Ahab has more than one gold coin!" someone calls out, and Josiah thinks he recognizes that voice. "Pull as if your lives depend upon it."

Josiah turns to look where the voice has come from. Rooted in the stern of his boat, though not at any oar, sits Ahab himself. He calls out: "The doubloon goes to that man, but if we lose the whale, there will be another coin. So, pull, pull."

Gold coin? Captain Ahab? Josiah is only surprised that he is not surprised. Of course, since this is Josiah's own dream, he is on one of the Pequod's *whaleboats.*

As the men pull even harder, Josiah shivers. He knows what the men do not know. He knows what the end of the hunt will be.

He looks around for Ishmael Black and cannot immediately identify him. He thinks: Does that mean Ishmael is a completely false messenger, and he never actually sailed on the *Pequod?* Or that he is back on the mother ship? In the kitchen as cook? Organizing Ahab's private library? In the brig as a prisoner? *Josiah does not know. All he can do now is watch, remember.*

Suddenly the man in front of the portside boat calls out frantically, "He's turning! The whale is turning!"

The starboard boatsman adds, "He's turned. He sees us. Ahab's doom is on his way."

"Then stand for it," *the harpooner on Josiah's boat cries out.* "We are three to the whale's one. Make your mark! Ready your harp!!!"

Josiah wonders why, when the whale had been far from them, no more than a white fluke and a towering white tail—the water betwixt the boats and the beast had appeared broken and chopped up. But now that the whale has turned swiftly in their direction, the closer he comes, the more the waves smooth out, as if a serene carpet has been set upon the brine. This seems counter to intuition, counter to knowledge, and yet it is so. It is all too sudden, between one breath and the next.

Then the whale rises up before them, his entire hump, so dazzlingly white, totally visible. Projecting from his back is a shattered lance. And from the lance, like blood flowing, are bright red ribbons.

"Ahab's old harpoon," Josiah says under his breath, knowing that to be true. He turns and looks back at the Pequod, *where presumably his father is standing, spyglass in hand, watching the harpoon boats, the rising whale. Where perhaps Ishmael Black waits, his hands on the cannibal's coffin, already working to save himself alone.*

Perhaps, Josiah thinks, perhaps he alone has been sent here to save his father, save them all, though he does not know how he can manage such a feat. Using the Quaker term, he muses: "More likely I am here to witness."

Witness. Go home with the news. "I alone am here to tell thee." As if the news would come more softly from his lips than the librarian's.

And then he thinks: Here is Ahab's Doom. *He sees Ahab himself, standing, raising his fist at the whale, calling to it, taunting it, tempting it, threatening it. Offering it life for life, death for death.*

No one on his boat pays Josiah even the smallest of attentions.

It is as if he does not exist for them. Certainly not in the way they exist for him.

But as much as Josiah sees of the whale above the water, he knows now how much more of the whale is buried beneath those strangely placid waves. And perhaps most fearsome of all, he knows how large the whale's wretched jaw is, that leviathan maw which even now rises above him in a bony arch.

He waits for the crush of it, the crack of doom.

He watches as angels rise up from the water on broad white wings, heading towards him with joyous cries, and he leaps up, meaning to say that angels are coming. But Josiah realizes at the last moment that they are herons being driven from the water by the giant whale on its way for retribution. And so instead, he cries out: "The birds! The birds!" But nobody hears him save one man, sitting in the back of the third boat, who turns with startled eyes to stare at him. That man is his father. Not safe on the big ship. But here, because he has to be, with the men. To save them if he can. To die with them if he must.

"Oh, Father," Josiah cries out, his arms flung wide. And his father hears, and is comforted.

Josiah looks over at the whale. Perhaps he can still stop the slaughter. "Moby-Dick," he says aloud, "I see thee. I truly see thee." And he does, that arch of jaw now open—Josiah sees down to the very end of the tale.

The whale stares right back at him, as if peeling him away from the rest of the men. As if recognizing Josiah is different, that he is ghosting in the boat.

*Then Moby-Dick's huge tail scythes through the water,
drowning all the boats.*

Josiah awoke, drenched not in seawater but sweat, realizing that in some odd fashion, without ever having
been on a whaling ship or one of the harpoon boats in
his life, he still must have been dreaming true because
it was all so real. He wiped his sleeve across his face,
and took a deep breath. He could feel his heart beating
twice as fast as before.

When he stood, Ezekiel stood with him, whining
a bit, as if he had been on the harpoon boat as well,
although he was probably just reacting to Josiah's
sweating, and the faulty rhythm of his boy's breathing.

"A dream, just a dream," Josiah whispered hoarsely
to the dog, though it had seemed so much more than
that. "Time to go back to our camp and try to salvage
meaning from this most disturbing dream."

Zeke barked once, then twice, turned as if he totally
understood, and started trotting through the arch,
and up and over the hill, leaving Josiah to find the way
back on his own.

CHAPTER FIFTEEN:
The Dog's Transcendence

There was no denying it. Josiah dawdled on the way back to the boat. The dream was too recent, too potent, too undecipherable, too real.

He wondered if he was losing his mind from the crack of the boom. Wondered if exhaustion, or too little food, or too much worry was clouding his judgment. Whether the big lunch meal, so unexpected, had been too much for his shrunken stomach and sent him spiraling into a fever.

He suddenly worried that he was being too harsh on his mother without knowing what her choices actually were, or too easy on his workload and not trying hard enough to get home.

Did he possibly see himself on an extended trip that would end . . . when it was over, and the weather turned cold? Or had he just given up hope of being rescued, or being able to rebuild his boat, or still being loved with his father gone and his mother . . . doing whatever?

And then he dismissed everything he'd just thought as *havering*. Making long-winded excuses for not doing all the necessary chores, something that sometimes bedeviled him at home.

And feeling foolish for not having a friend to talk to on the island who could really talk back. Just a dog.

Most of all, he blamed himself for having been a fool in the first place, getting into a boat without a chart, or proper provisions, or any sort of plan. And for taking this long to figure that much out.

By the time he had excoriated himself thoroughly, he was exhausted, angry, and guilt-ridden, the dream under the arch all but forgotten.

He crested the hill, expecting to just go back and find their extra food, settle down for dinner, even have an early evening with Zeke.

Suddenly, he heard a terrible noise.

Not the wind, not the waves, not even a storm coming. Those would have been expected, even acceptable. But as he came in sight of the boat, he realized there was a high scream in the air, a cry of an animal in distress.

He glanced around, trying to pinpoint the site of

the scream, and saw Zeke halfway off the island, being pulled into the water by some kind of creature that had him by the foot.

Shark? Josiah thought. *Whale? Tide?*

Screeching back, Josiah began to run towards Zeke as the dog went deeper in, now up to his stomach, all the while trying to savage something with his teeth and growling at his failure.

"Ezekiel—To me! To me!" Josiah screamed, which under ordinary circumstances would have worked. In fact, Zeke tried to turn, but it soon became clear that something had a serious hold on him. And clearer, still, when the something's head and back rose up out of the water.

It was a seal, not fully grown, and probably not the initial aggressor. That had surely been Zeke himself. A young seal, especially a small one like that, would not have attacked unless fighting back.

"Stupid dog, let it go!" he cried to Zeke, flinging a piece of driftwood at the seal's head.

It missed, but Zeke flinched, and his momentary distraction only gave the seal time for one last haul on his leg before Josiah reached the shore and ran straight into the incoming tide.

Grabbing the knife from the sheath, which he'd had pushed into his trousers waistband for the walk back, Josiah battled the water to get to Zeke's side, striking downward in the direction where he could just about see the gray body of the seal.

This was not as easy to do as he'd hoped. The water resisted quite a bit. But by pushing harder, he felt the knife connect with flesh. Just not as strongly as he had intended. He prayed it was the seal and not the dog he had wounded.

Suddenly Zeke backed up, free of whatever had held him, and fled onto the shore, far enough away, but limping badly and favoring his left paw.

Forgetting all about being a Quaker and a pacifist, Josiah struck one more blow with the knife, which glanced off the seal's flipper before the seal swam free. That left Josiah winded, but relieved, even though his heart was drumming hard against his chest.

He turned to Zeke, now crouching on the ground, moaning, and licking his forepaw frantically as if trying to clean it.

"Let me see that," Josiah said to the cringing dog, before realizing he was shouting. He modulated his voice, almost whispering, "Ezekiel, let me see thy paw."

There was some blood, though most had been washed away by the sea, and there was a slash on the pad of the foot that looked quite deep, which would make walking difficult for a while.

He bent over, then picked up the dog, stumbling because Zeke was no lightweight, even though they had both lost pounds on the island from lack of proper meals.

Then, staggering toward the boat, he brought his injured companion to safety.

By this time Zeke was trembling from both shock and cold, so Josiah first wrapped him in the heavy coat and rocked him like a child, a very big, furry child, until Zeke had completely calmed down. Only then did Josiah look closely at the paw. It would need something to keep it from getting grit in the wound, and it would also need proper washing out. He had no medicines to treat it, no salves or bandages. His only hope was to keep the wound clean. So, he cut off part of his right-hand sleeve with the knife and wrapped the rather ragged piece of cloth securely around Zeke's injured foot, knotting the ends.

Then he rolled Zeke under *Petrel*, tying him there to the small anchor with one of the ropes they had found in the fisherman's shack, leaving him with the coat as a bed.

"Stay!" Josiah said sternly, one of the few commands the dog knew. Then, to be sure, he put his right hand up sternly. "Ezekiel, stay!"

Standing, he announced—as if the dog could understand—"I have to get fresh water to wash thy wound again later, and then start the fire and heat up the rest of the food, so thee must remain here."

He worried that Zeke might still try to follow and kept looking back.

But either the dog understood the solemnity of the command, or he was just too exhausted to disobey. Or else he knew in his doggy way that standing with his foot bound and hurting was too much a shock to follow wherever Josiah planned to go. Not to mention, he had an anchor tied to his foot.

And to make certain that neither the seal nor its mother, father, or older sibling could come anywhere near to assault Zeke again, Josiah lowered the boat completely over him. Zeke made no complaint.

Only then did Josiah head out to get the water. He thought it also made sense to pick up some more clams on the way so he wouldn't feel the need to leave Zeke the next day to find them food. Of course, having already raided the close-by clam beds, he had to wade farther along the coast till he came to another good scattering of shellfish.

Taking off his shoes and stockings, still damp from his rescue of Zeke, he rolled up his pants legs over his knees, then slid down the dune into the fresh water to gather the clams, placing them up on the edge of the beach where he could collect them later.

When he had counted about two dozen, both littleneck clams and the bigger ones, he thought it enough for a really nice meal, another celebration, really. And shrugging out of his shirt again, this time to use it as a carry bag, he looked at the shirt and shook his head, thinking: *It will soon be in threads, which is fine as long as it is summer, but . . .*

He had just gotten back into his shoes and stockings when he saw something he hadn't seen on the island before.

Nestled in a patch of gravelly ground well above the sea line was a bird's nest. Quietly, he went over to it. There were no birds on the nest or anywhere in sight, but it contained two smallish eggs. They were both a pale buff color, with some very subtle black markings, as if a traveling artist had spattered paint on them.

Eggs, he thought. *What a gift!* He couldn't stop grinning. One of his jobs at home was to gather the chicken eggs each morning for breakfast. And if there were extra, his mother used them to make breads or cakes. He could boil these in the half-bailer, and what a feast *that* would be!

Chickens laid their eggs every day. They didn't seem to mind that the eggs were gone when they returned to the nests. They just laid more. Perhaps this bird, whatever kind it was, would do the same.

Gathering the two eggs with great care, he placed them on top of the clams before walking slowly back to the camp.

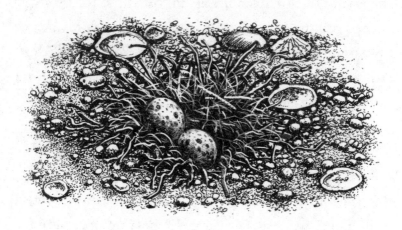

That night, after he and Zeke had eaten their clams, Josiah boiled the eggs till they were hard enough but not too hard. Once they were cooled down, he knocked each against one of the rocks, then carefully peeled them. He ate one egg, Zeke the other, both washing them down with fresh water.

Josiah was pretty sure Zeke fell asleep first. But he woke before the dog and felt, for the first time, as if they were truly going to be able to get through the next few weeks of hard work on the boat and make it home.

Chapter Sixteen:
The Idyll Is Over

Upon waking, Josiah knew that he had to make a plan. The boat was neither seaworthy nor sail-worthy—if *sail-worthy* was in fact a word. He might have just made it up. He would need nails to hold the two planks in place. He would need needle and thread to resew the torn sails. He would have to provision the boat with food that would still be edible when cold.

Perhaps they could make it back to Nantucket in a day. He had probably come to this No Man's Island in that time. Much of it when knocked out. But even if he fixed everything, he could not count on a proper wind, or the keel's ability to keep them afloat, or its sails to hold the wind. He could not dismiss the awful possibility of the boat sinking, or even breaking up on another shore.

Indeed, he did not actually know where he was

without compass or charts. Did not know whether he was above the Vineyard or below. Or off the charts entirely. There was no way for him to tell. After all, he'd been unconscious for a good part of the time the boat had been on her way to this misbegotten isle.

But I will try! Not for myself, but for Mother's sake, my father's memory, and Zeke's safety.

Josiah knew he had gotten them into this mess, and it was up to him to get them out. His father would expect—*would have* expected—him to do that. And he would not let his own follies besmirch his father's memory. And he now understood he could not let his mother continue to mourn for two.

Rolling out from under the boat, he gave his shoulders a bit of a shake. Then he glanced at the boat's bottom, where the two missing boards had been. One board was still standing upright, like a statue, at the prow of the boat, where it had plowed in on their first landing. The other was on its side nearby. He checked them both.

The upright board was missing four nails, the other six. That meant he would need ten nails at the very least, and there were probably only two places on the island to find anything he could use. One was at the fisherman's shack, the other in the masses of driftwood he had brought onto the shore over the weeks here, using them for the fire with which he cooked their food as well as stockpiling firewood against the cold days to come.

As he walked over to the haphazard pile of wood, he realized for the first time how stupidly he had prepared for a long stay. Like a child living a fairy tale, not a young man thinking like a shipwrecked mariner.

This time, he began by separating the pieces of wood. On one side, he set bark, tree limbs, and small bits of unidentified wood useful only for the fire. But anything that looked as if it had been shaped by a man's hand, he set down on the other side.

By the time an hour had gone by, which Josiah knew by checking the sun's travel overhead, he had looked through everything in his haphazard wood pile. He'd located only two man-made items—what looked to be a drawer, possibly from a ship's cabin, and half a door. The sum of the usable hardware came to seven nails, one bolt, and two screws. It was a start. But only a small one. There would be no room for mistakes.

Next, he removed the pieces of sail he had stowed in the prow of the ship. They were filthy and full of mold. They would all have to be washed and dried in the sun before he could possibly see well enough what needed sewing, and what was useless and had to be thrown away.

It took another two hours or more for him to wade onto the shoals and scrub the pieces of sail with his bare hands. Then he set them on top of the boat's keel to dry.

It turned out there were too many sheets and not enough keel. He spread the largest of the pieces on grassy areas near the boat. It might take several days before he could actually try to sew them together.

He knew little of sewing but had watched enough sailors working on the sheets of various boats. Of course, they were each well-equipped with tough thread and good needles, and each owned a sailmaker's palm. He had only his marlinspike to poke sewing holes through the tough canvas. He had netting he would have to cannibalize for thread. As for the sailmaker's palm, that palm-sized leather shield with the metal eye that saved many a sailor's hand from injury while doing the heavy sewing on canvas sails, he would have to think about that later.

It was growing towards midday when he had finished washing the sheets and was ready to head out for the shack. Though he was pretty certain he had already removed everything of use from it, and that had been little enough. Just the fisherman's coat, with its pocket surprise, and a tangle of rope nets.

Glancing at the sky again, he noted a small easterly wind, a few clouds. It would be a good day to explore the shack and then the eastern side of the island where the channel rushed by, looking for wood. Every day something else drifted in. There might be more wood with nails floating about, and perhaps one last surprise in the shack that he might use for the trip.

For now, he would leave Zeke sleeping. The dog's injured paw would only slow the two of them down.

So, with his leather knife-and-marlinspike carrier, plus the striker, in case he needed a hammer, or to make a fire, and the larger of the two bailers, he walked quietly away from the camp.

He felt somehow liberated from fear, from the endless little chores that had been keeping the two of them alive. Liberated from grief, and from thoughts of failure. He would fix the boat, sew the sails, and limp back home. Or die.

That last thought, once in his mind, would not leave him. But as a sailor's son, he had lived with that constant specter every time he—or his father—had stepped onto the deck of a boat. Though nobody spoke about it, nobody planned for it, it was there and, they all knew, in God's hands.

God's hands, he thought angrily, *but not mine. Well, I*

shall put as much as I can into my own hands this time.
He walked on, the wind feathering his hair.

The hill under the midday sun looked a bit daunting, higher than usual, as if it had grown overnight, but the fisherman's shack on hilltop loomed like an un-opened present. Josiah knew he had gone through it thoroughly and had few expectations. He no longer believed in fairy tales. Still, he did not waste time getting there, though he was huffing by the top of the hill.

He opened the door and glanced in, unsurprised that it was bare. After all, hadn't *he* been the one to empty it out? But now he was looking for usable nails, not another coat or nets, or even a striker. Those had all been provided already.

He worked his way around the shack carefully, both inside and out, noting a few possible nails he might withdraw from the door and the side boards, plus two screws from the handles. It could be done without destroying the shack itself, which he meant to leave as a present to any person who might wreck upon the rocks of the island. Or a thank-you to the unknown fisherman, should he return.

All in all, he found a possible ten nails, bringing his

total to seventeen, thus giving himself a bit of wiggle room on the rebuilding of the boat's bottom.

Taking out the leather sheath with the knife and marlinspike, he began the work of removing the nails, mentally preparing himself for another hour or two of hard work.

He was surprised at how easily the first three nails came out, but the rest were the struggle he had anticipated, and the last two were much too twisted to come out at all. So that made not seventeen but fifteen nails, still giving him some leeway on the re-boarding of the keel.

He was congratulating himself, and just putting the nails into the bailer for safekeeping, when an odd grunting sound made him turn around swiftly, knife in hand.

Zeke was within a few feet of him, laboring up the last few inches of the hill, favoring his injured foot, which was now trailing a bit of torn cloth. How he had scrambled out from under the lowered boat, how he had pulled loose from both rope and anchor, would remain a mystery.

"Silly dog!" Josiah said aloud. The fondness in his voice did not give away his distress that the dog's tracking him to the shack might have reopened the wound. Not to mention filling it with grass bits and sand.

He needed Zeke to be strong for the trip home.

"Sit! Sit *down*! Thee should not be on thy sore paw."

Zeke did not sit, but rather struggled up the last few inches of hill before sticking his head into the shack and sniffing around, as if he didn't expect Josiah to have done a thorough-enough job of checking the shack out.

"Stop!" Josiah commanded. "There's nothing there, Ezekiel." Now there was even more annoyance in his voice. "Sit. Down!" He made one of the few hand signals the dog understood, then commanded even louder: "Sit!"

But Zeke continued farther into the shack, not shrinking from his self-appointed work. Suddenly he began digging frantically on the far corner of the floor, which was only a dark patch of wood and sand. He tore up the dirt, getting his wounded paw filthy in the process.

"Out! Out!" Josiah cried, dragging the dog by his leather collar and pulling him out of the shack.

Zeke had something in his mouth, growling at it, or at Josiah. It was hard to tell which.

"Oh, drop that filthy thing!" Josiah said, and this time Zeke obeyed.

It was not—as Josiah first feared—the remnants of some kind of dead animal. A rat was his first thought. A gull his second. But as he poked at it with the striker, he realized it was not an animal at all, but a nest of twisted cuttyhunk fibers, made of linen threads, possibly once a net or a rug, though it looked as if some animal over the years had used it as a nest.

There were certainly holes enough in the shack's flooring to have allowed some creature to come in to shelter in the winter. And that made Josiah think that no one had visited the shack in at least a year, maybe two. Maybe more.

Immediately realizing this was the shack's last gift, and a good one at that, he praised his dog. All the while his mind was figuring that if he plucked off the rotten parts, if he washed the filth off thoroughly and untwisted the strands, they would be the best kind of sturdy linen thread for repairing the sails. Much better than destroying one of the coarser fishing nets.

"Good dog," Josiah said, kneeling and sticking his nose into Zeke's furry neck. "Thee has saved me a second time."

He put the rest of the filthy cuttyhunk into the bailer atop the nails, and the two of them walked back to the boat, but slowly because of Zeke's foot.

Zeke slept the rest of the afternoon while Josiah untwisted and washed the cuttyhunk fibers, and straightened out the nails from the shack with the striker on a convenient and fairly flat granite rock nearby.

———————

Because he didn't want to chance Zeke making another long walk, Josiah used the largest of the fishing nets to try and gather some fish for dinner within sight of the boat, tying pieces of old clam to the strings, while Zeke slept away the afternoon.

The lucky day continued, and Josiah was able to serve up four small smelt and a flounder, which he cooked over a slow fire in the larger bailer. A delicious meal for them both.

Then, before going to sleep, he turned over all the sails to let them dry out on the other side, because he could smell no rain in the air.

"Though to be fair," he whispered to the snoring dog, "after the heavy smell of cooking fish, I might not have been able to sniff even the greatest of winds."

Zeke made no answer. He didn't even stir. And soon Josiah's snores joined him in the shelter of the boat, where they slept well-fed, and dreamless, until the morning.

CHAPTER SEVENTEEN:
Days of Fixing

That next week was, as Josiah finally admitted, the hardest days of work in his entire life. And at fourteen he had already worked hard at home as the man of the house when his father was away at sea. In addition, because of his mother's catarrh, he also had to clean the house, keep watch on the chickens, care for the garden, and make sure his boat was in shape during the long, cold winter. Oh, and milk the cow. He hated that cow, all grunts and farts and kicks when he milked her.

And, of course, he still had to attend school. This was to be his next to final year, unless he went off island for a university. He was no longer sure he wanted to be a sailor.

So, hard work wasn't new to him. Here on the island, going clamming and fishing every day just to feed himself and the dog seemed but a small extension beyond the work he had had to do at home. But it wasn't the work that bothered him, it was the loneliness, the uncertainty of the life, a need for comfort with a word—not just a lick on the hand or the chin from his dog—that he longed for.

Still, nothing had prepared him for these last few days' work, because he knew it was a life-and-death occupation. If he did not do things correctly, it could mean death for both Zeke and himself. Either in a compromised boat or over a miserable and short last few weeks on the tiny island.

Surprisingly, the easiest part of the boat work had been the hammering back of the two boards into the keel, though Josiah had to make a second and third trip to the shack to hack out three more nails, since several had been bent beyond saving, when he tried to hammer them in with the firestriker.

The boat, now, a day into this second work week, was, he hoped, truly waterproof, tight, and ready. Though he had not set the mast back in yet. But the sail, alas, was not in good shape at all. And he certainly wouldn't get far with one lone oar.

It turned out that sewing the sail was a much more

difficult and labor-intensive job than straightening or hammering in nails and turning screws. Plus, while hammering boards was a skill his father had shown him how to do, and often enough to make a difference, he thought that his father may not even have known how to properly sew a sail himself.

On land, sewing was mostly a woman's occupation. Except for tailors, of course, and the sailmakers in their loft in Nantucket, which he and his father had visited several times. But to Josiah, watching men hard at work sewing had seemed odd, almost unmanly, though as his father had noted gently, "Without their work, how could we sailors be certain to get home?"

How indeed!

On board the big ships there were always at least one if not more designated sailmakers who had heavy needles, a measuring device, and proper thread. Plus, the ever-necessary sailmaker's palm.

Here on the island, Josiah had had to create everything from scratch.

He had known fixing the boat wasn't going to be easy. That was already understood. But fixing sails had never looked like such hard work. Yet it turned out to be *extremely* hard, grinding, even punishing work, especially if one was without proper needles and thread.

First, though, it took a couple of days to wash, dry, and then untangle the linen nest into enough usable,

individual strands. And once they were ready, and as clean as he could make them, he had to find a way to poke the right-size holes in the cloth for the linen thread.

He had only the marlinspike for that. Which meant hours of rotating the spike between aching palms until there were enough well-placed small and workable holes punched through the reluctant canvas. After that he had to push the even-more reluctant thread through each hole bit by bit.

By the end of the first hour, his palms were so bruised by trying to push the thread through he had to stop for the day and fashion for himself a makeshift but, in the end, quite usable sailmaker's palm.

It turned out the leather sheath that used to house knife and marlinspike gave him the best option. It wasn't perfect, but it helped. He fixed the strap, opened it up to fit his hand, then with marlinspike and striker working together, he made a couple of holes to sew the strap into its new configuration. Not elegant, but definitely useful.

The first thread that he managed to push through a hole worked, and he eagerly began pushing it through a second, nearby hole, then nearly cried when it slipped out of both because he hadn't known he had to knot the end.

So, he rethought the steps, remembering every time

to knot the individual thread's end, or else all the hard work on those stitches would slip out.

Sometimes this meant not only double-knotting but triple-knotting, depending on the size of the hole he had made. And then it took two days to perfect the steps so that he didn't have to think about doing the knotting with every new thread, but did it instinctively every time.

However, even with his hand-built sailmaker's palm, at the end of each sewing day, his hands were covered in sore spots that made clamming and fishing more difficult, though of course, that had to be done as well.

Everything slowed down because of the work. Everything except the march of days that turned into weeks that began to slip towards autumn.

Yes, Josiah was exhausted. He tried hard not to let it slow him down.

By the end of the first week, Zeke's paw seemed completely healed, but his need to be a companion for the hunt for food became more insistent. "Whereas, *my* paw . . ." Josiah grumbled, holding up his right hand with its red and blue blotches. The dog did not answer him.

Luckily another bird and her mate (or perhaps it was

the same one; Josiah was never to know) had begun laying in the nest again, and so he was able to supplement meals with boiled eggs every few days. Much easier and drier to collect and cook than fish or clams.

Josiah soon learned to work on the sails in the morning and again in the early evening when the sun was not at its hottest, which helped his exhaustion somewhat. But it took a full two weeks to fix the sail, much of it undoing and redoing what he'd already done. He learned a lot about sewing along the way, but it was speed that he would have preferred perfecting, and that he never did.

The patches he sewed, even by his own reckoning, were ugly and inelegant, even though they held. A real sailmaker would have made them much better, even under the same harsh conditions. A real sailor would never have used such a sail.

But he had some hope the ugly sheets would do the job. They *had* to. He had no other tools. Or skills. Or another sail to use instead. He only had *need* to drive him on.

He hoped the salvaged sail, ill-sewn as it was, would still hold the wind. At least as far as Nantucket. However far that was.

"And," he said solemnly to Zeke, "I will never un-
derestimate a sailmaker again."

At the end of the second week, when Josiah raised
the sail to check it out on the mast, he had to admit
that the higher the sail went up, the better it looked.
It was still clearly not professionally patched, but his
sad attempt at herringbone stitches were no longer as
visible. And the linen thread almost blended in with
the not-quite clean sail.

He lowered the sail again, and to celebrate, he
walked with Zeke to the arch of bone, to sit for a
while and contemplate their next move. He wanted to
think about what his father might have done differently if marooned on an island. Surely not sit around
for weeks clamming and netting the occasional fish.
Or moaning about life. Surely he would have tried to
save his men, if any had been with him. Or his dog.
And surely he would have immediately found a way
to get back home to his wife and son.

The dog stirred by his side as if to say, "But thee
saved *me*."

"We saved each other," Josiah said to Zeke, as Zeke
moved closer, putting his head in Josiah's lap.

The arch of bone at Josiah's back was solid. This

time he leaned into it, ready for a dream, though now not sure that with all his work and self-discovery, he hadn't outgrown the need for them.

"A true captain of the sea would surely have done things differently, fixed his boat quickly, left here early on," Josiah whispered, as both he and Zeke lapsed into sleep.

At once Josiah began dreaming about the *Pequod*. He did not know it then, but it would be his final full dream under the Arch of Bone.

Dream Four:
Oh, My Noble Soul

*T*he boat is not as shipshape as the last time he saw it. Though the day is a clear, steel blue, the sea rolling, but not yet tossed by any whale's tale. There is a dark smell as if the ship has pores that are leaking oil everywhere. The deck is not clean. It has a gloss of what might be blood, though it is black. It looks as if the sailors have painted the deck with death and then disappeared down below to sing songs of their own resurrection.

The sight of the empty deck, the black boards, makes Josiah shiver with fear, though whether it is his dream-self shivering or his actual self, or both, he cannot tell. He only knows this is a dream, but it is true, too.

He sees his father coming onto the deck through an un-marked door, heading towards the lee side of the ship, and Josiah follows.

There, staring down into the tide, is old Ahab. He is unmistakable because of his bone-white peg leg, but also this is the third time Josiah has seen him, and the captain's outfit does not change from dream to dream.

Nor does his bone leg.

On hearing footsteps and the clearing of a throat behind him, Captain Ahab turns.

Josiah realizes he looks much older than last time, more twisted. His face is a chart of wrinkles, his eyes like coals glowing in the ashes of ruin. Or perhaps the sun is hitting him too hard in the face, some kind of punishment for what is about to happen. Or has already happened. Perhaps this is a ghost ship.

One cannot trust time in dreams.

"Starbuck!" Ahab says. It is a command to come closer.

"Sir!" Josiah and his father answer in voices so similar, it is as if they speak with one voice. Josiah instantly realizes his mistake. But the captain never flicks a glance in his direction. Clearly Ahab believes he is speaking only to the older Starbuck. That there is no boy there within his gaze.

Josiah thinks: I am invisible to both men. Just as I was invisible in the harpoon boat where only the whale truly saw me. *It is dream logic. Or magic. He is not certain which.*

The captain starts talking about his first whale kill as a young harpooner. Only eighteen years old. And Josiah thinks: Dying men talk like this, not someone on a fresh chase. *Perhaps Ahab will turn the ship around. Perhaps he will forget about the whale. Perhaps there is already enough oil to satisfy the owners, for surely it is leaking from every seam in the ship.*

And then he thinks: Perhaps the ship did not go down, and Ishmael Black was but a rogue sailor, throwing the coffin over the ship's side and saving only himself.

Now the old man is talking about how he has been in this life too long. "Oh, weariness," he says. "Heaviness!" He groans.

He leans towards the older Starbuck as if making a confession. "Forty years I have fed on dry salted fare—fit emblem of the dry nourishment of my soul." He stops, clearly musing a bit more, than adds: "I see my wife and child in thine eye." He shakes his head as if denying the vision, which makes his gray hair look like a wave tossing.

Not dying, *Josiah thinks.* Already dead.

"Sir!" Josiah's father says. "I shall follow the beast. Thee need not go after it."

"No, no, stay on board." Captain Ahab holds up his hands. "Lower not when I chase the white whale. That hazard is mine alone."

Josiah cries out, "Father, tell him it is no man's hazard. Tell him he is the father to all the men on the ship as thee art father to me."

His father looks around as if he has heard Josiah, and then he says, "Oh, my noble soul. Why should anyone give chase to that hated fish? Let us all fly these deadly waters."

However, the captain has turned back to gaze at the sea, this time as if looking down into a watery grave. And now he points a shaking finger at a raised white fountain of water. "Thar! Thar she blows!" And then he calls out to the bosun to lower the boats for the chase. As he has clearly done a hundred times. As he will clearly do a hundred times more.

When Josiah turns back, he sees his father, shoulders rounded in despair, stealing away, and he shouts after him, "Why does thee not task him again, Father? Speak thy truth to that power. It is in thy hands now. Save the ship and all its brave men!"

But Josiah knows the answer to that. His father is a good husband. A good father. A good man. And a trusted second-in-command. A Quaker, he has said his piece. Offered himself in the captain's place. He can do no more but trust in Providence. A Providence that does not hear him.

And besides, it is too late for any such thoughts.

Ishmael Black told the truth. Father will never get home. But I, *Josiah thinks,* I can.

He woke to a sunset full of beauty and danger, and a sky that threatened rain. Zeke woke at the same time.

They hurried back to the catboat, not even stopping to clam or check the plover's nest. By the time they arrived, they were soaking wet. The newly turned boat had an inch of rainwater from the cloudburst, which made it clear that both planks had held fast, but the boat had to be set again on its side to drain, and the sails would get muddy again unless they got them off, a laborious business that took another half hour.

By then, the ground was soaked as well, and Josiah moved the boat away from the worst of the wetness. When it was finally drained, he turned it fully on its other side, placing the sails over the keel in an attempt to keep them reasonably clean. "Another washing," he said to Zeke, "cannot hurt."

Zeke looked unimpressed.

Then the two of them crawled under the boat, exhausted, wrapped in the fisherman's coat which kept them somewhat, but not completely, dry during the night, because the rain came from down hard enough to creep under the boat in a steady stream.

This time, Josiah slept without dreams. However, Zeke seemed to be chasing something in his own dreams all night long, for his legs moved ceaselessly throughout the night. He woke uneasily to see his boy rolling out from under the boat, watched him turn, sit up, and stretch under a bleak new dawn.

CHAPTER EIGHTEEN:
Promises

Josiah looked at the dog, who seemed to be having trouble waking.

"I want to make thee some promises, Zeke," he said.

Suddenly alert, the dog sat up, bumping his head slightly on the boat. Then, settling a bit, he stretched out, ears up, tail wagging. He looked adoringly at Josiah. This, *this* was the boy he recognized.

"*Promise one*: we are going to put together a lot of cooked food."

At the word "food," Zeke's tail made wider waves in the air.

"*Promise two*: I will go over every bit of the boat a second and third time to make sure she's seaworthy."

Josiah grinned at his dog.

Zeke responded to the grin with more tail movement and a bit of a bark. He was not responding to the promise, of course. Josiah knew that, but the dog's sudden good mood was encouraging, to say the least.

"*Promise three,*" Josiah said. "I will check the weather as best I can. We will not leave in a storm. We will not leave until we have the best weather possible. But we *will* leave soon. Not today, possibly not tomorrow. But when I am certain we are ready."

Josiah stood and so did the dog, prancing about, waiting for something to be thrown. Feeling momentarily indulgent, Josiah picked up several sticks and flung them one at a time in three different directions, calling out each time, "Promise one, promise two, promise three!"

Zeke brought all three sticks back one at a time and laid each reverently at Josiah's feet as if they were his promises, too.

Of course, it being New England, it rained constantly for the next three days. Josiah did not leave the shelter of the overturned boat, except for going fishing in the nude, making a run for fresh water, and out twice a day to pee. He built a small fire underneath the boat each day, just enough to boil the cod and two smelt.

Josiah told Zeke all the nursery rhymes and fairy tales he could remember, and the dog didn't know or care when he repeated five or six of his own favorites when he'd run out.

They slept a lot, too, the drumming on the boat's hull overhead the perfect lullaby.

On the fourth day the sun came up smiling so broadly it seemed as if they had moved to the Antipodes.

It took all of Josiah's promises to himself to keep working, first testing the catboat's seaworthiness by dragging it into the high tide and paddling it around parts of the island until he was satisfied with how she handled.

The sail occupied him for the next three days. Some of it needed resewing. And some of what he had to do was to test old skills in a different way—getting the mast and sails up when neither were perfect.

But the boat and sail would do, or at least it was the best *Josiah* could do.

Now all he had left to accomplish was gather enough clams and fish and eggs to cook and store in the bailer and the pail. He hoped that they would not need to bail out the boat before the first meal in had been eaten.

———————

The next day dawned gray and unreadable. Josiah did not dare attempt a voyage that might end in disaster. Instead he and Zeke took a walk about the island, finding another nest of two eggs. "Dinner!" he announced to Zeke, who barked his joy.

A while later, Josiah found that the scrubby bushes he had noted weeks before were really blueberry bushes. The gulls had already stripped the top part bare, but there were still berries to be had, and he grabbed those while Zeke barked away the frantic gulls.

"Dessert!" he said, but Zeke, still waiting for the first course, did not respond.

As they came back, they walked through the Arch of Bones. Josiah did not want to chance another dream in case it was a warning not to leave.

So, he did not sit down but instead stretched out his arm and placed his hand lightly on the left side of the arch, directly on the bone.

Suddenly he found himself stretch-legged across a wooden box that was fighting through large waves. Looking down, he saw strange carvings across the face of the box and realized that this was a coffin.

I am Ishmael, *he thought. And then he smiled wryly, saying aloud,* "And I will get back to Mother."

He lifted his hand from the jawbone, and the dream stopped at once. Then he whistled for Zeke, and they took off towards the boat, and the next day's long journey home.

Coda

It was a fine day, the wind southwesterly. The boat handled well enough, if a bit sluggish. She leaked a bit, too, but not much. Nothing the bailer couldn't handle.

The turn at the end of the desolate island was only slightly fraught, and Josiah's stomach ached in anticipation. But he managed it like an old hand. In a mild wind like this, the jibe was no real challenge, and he knew it.

"A canny sailor," the harbormaster had called Josiah. A canny sailor Josiah vowed he would be.

However, Zeke kept his nose firmly in the cuddy. He would have been just as happy to have stayed longer on the little isle. Maybe forever. As long as a boat trip wasn't part of the plan.

As they sailed away from the island, going easterly, Josiah realized how truly small a place it was, and riding low in the water. A bigger blow in the winter, and it would possibly have been *under*water a few inches or even a few feet. Probably why the shack had been located up on the hill. But they moved swiftly in the steady breeze, and the islet was soon out of sight.

As they sailed a bit farther on an easterly course, Josiah could suddenly see a second island ahead.

For a moment, his heart pounded. Was it Nantucket? So soon? Had they suffered for so many weeks when help was that near at hand?

But the closer they came, the more he realized it was just another small island lined up with theirs, slightly more substantial, and not as low. He thought it looked vaguely familiar, but didn't dare chance a stop there because the shoals and rocks looked fierce, and he saw no easy harbor. Also, he saw no sign of habitation, though it was certainly not as barren as his isle had been. At least here were actual trees. And bushes. A lot of bushes. Which might have meant more food.

Only bad luck, it seemed, had grounded him on the poorer island. Or maybe good luck, since there had been the fisherman's shack. And the Arch of Bone.

And smaller shoals and rocks to get away from. He would never know which.

He reached into the bailer and took out a boiled egg for them each, peeled them both, and he and Zeke ate them for lunch.

It took two more hours before a large island came in sight. Josiah realized at once that it was the northwest corner of Nantucket. He began to shake. Zeke came over and laid his head in Josiah's lap, whining.

It had been so close, so close. He felt tears spring into his eyes and wiped them quickly away. And yet, without a working boat, he and Zeke would never have been able to leave the isle.

"Oh, Mother!" he said. "Oh, Father!" Whether it was a cry of thanks or relief or sorrow, or a plea for forgiveness, he did not know.

He saw a shepherd in the meadow with a flock of ewes and a dog. He waved and Zeke barked. The dog turned to look at them but not the man. For a moment Josiah wondered if he was as invisible as any dream creature. Or as any dead man.

Then he said aloud, "No! I am in charge now. Our safety, our very lives are in my hands." He looked up at the sky. There was no lightning bolt to tell him nay.

At his boy's voice, Zeke gave a huge bark of approval. At that, the shepherd's dog barked back, and the man turned, saw them, and waved.

Josiah smiled. "That shepherd knows a Nantucket boy when he sees one, Zeke. We're almost home. We should be there by evening."

He expected a warm welcome from his mother who loved him and surely trusted he was alive, despite his long absence and her fears.

Hand on the tiller, the wind high in the patchworked sail, his head truly cleared, the chart in his heart showing the way, Josiah Starbuck set his course straight for home, where supper would be waiting and still hot.

J ane Yolen (*Owl Moon, The Midnight Circus,* the *How Do Dinosaurs* series)'s four-hundredth book came out this year, and she is starting the new count with *Arch of Bone*—with her eye on five hundred! She has been writing and publishing since the early sixties, when she sold her first book (about female pirates) on her twenty-second birthday. But Yolen began her publishing career as a journalist (short-lived) and as an editor (longer-lived), for Knopf and Harcourt, in the children's department.

Yolen graduated from Smith College in Northampton, Massachusetts, with an MEd (Master's degree in education) from the University of Massachusetts, Amherst. She has six honorary doctorates for her body of work. She was the first woman to give the Andrew

Lang lecture at St Andrews University in Scotland, in a lecture series that began in 1927. Yolen was also president for two years of the Science Fiction Writers of America, and on the board of the Society of Children's Book Writers for forty-five years.

Yolen's books and stories have won three World Fantasy Awards, two Nebula Awards, three Mythopoeic Awards, two Christopher Medals, three SCBWI awards, the Massachusetts Book Center Award, two Golden Kite Awards, and a Caldecott Medal as well many others. She was nominated in 2020 by the United States for the Astrid Lindgren Award. She was the first Western Mass author to win a New England Public Radio Arts and Humanities Award.

Yolen has also received awards from both the Jewish Book Council and the Catholic Book Council, making her very ecumenical. Her award from the Boston Science Fiction Association set her good coat on fire, which she takes as a lesson about the dangers of awards.

Yolen lives in Western Massachusetts and St Andrews, Scotland.

orn in the small town of Monson, Massachusetts, **Ruth Sanderson** has been a professional illustrator since 1975, with over eighty published children's books, in addition to illustrated book covers, fantasy art, collector's plates, animation concept art, and product design. Her illustrations credits include a famous edition of *Heidi* with one hundred full-color oil paintings as well as editions of *The Secret Garden*, *The Sleeping Beauty*, *The Twelve Dancing Princesses*, and many more. Sanderson teaches writing and illustrating for children in a summer graduate program at Hollins University in Roanoke, Virginia. She is a longtime member of the Society of Children's Book Writers and Illustrators and the Western Massachusetts Illustrators Guild. She last collaborated with Jane Yolen in 2000, illustrating *Where Have The Unicorns Gone?* (Simon & Schuster). Find more about Ruth Sanderson and her work at goldenwoodstudio.com.